Married! The word shot through her and made her shiver.

Was she really going to do this? Could she go through with it? Was she really going to marry this incredibly handsome man sitting beside her—this man she hardly knew? It looked like she was.

But before they tied the knot, there was something Kyra wanted to get out in the open—and hopefully put to rest. "What if...if you decide you like me too much?"

James's eyebrows rose quizzically. "What do you mean?"

She took a deep breath and contemplated another gulp of water. "I mean, I thought we'd agreed that this was not going to be a...a sexual arrangement."

"No, of course not." But a slow smile was beginning to curl the corners of his wide mouth. "Unless, of course, we both decide..."

Dear Reader,

From the enchantment of first loves to the wonder of second chances, Silhouette Romance demonstrates the power of genuine emotion. This month we continue our yearlong twentieth anniversary celebration with another stellar lineup, including the return of beloved author Dixie Browning with *Cinderella's Midnight Kiss*.

Next, Raye Morgan delivers a charming marriage-of-convenience story about a secretary who is *Promoted—To Wife!* And Silhouette Romance begins a new theme-based promotion, AN OLDER MAN, which highlights stories featuring sophisticated older men who meet their matches in younger, inexperienced women. Our premiere title is *Professor and the Nanny* by reader favorite Phyllis Halldorson.

Bestselling author Judy Christenberry unveils her new miniseries, THE CIRCLE K SISTERS, in *Never Let You Go.* When a millionaire businessman wins an executive assistant at an auction, he discovers that he wants her to be *Contractually His*...forever. Don't miss this conclusion of Myrna Mackenzie's THE WEDDING AUCTION series. And in Karen Rose Smith's *Just the Husband She Chose,* a powerful attorney is reunited in a marriage meant to satisfy a will.

In coming months, look for new miniseries by some of your favorite authors. It's an exciting year for Silhouette Books, and we invite you to join the celebration!

Happy reading!

Mary-Theresa Hussey

Mary-Theresa Hussey
Senior Editor

Please address questions and book requests to:
Silhouette Reader Service
U.S.: 3010 Walden Ave., P.O. Box 1325, Buffalo, NY 14269
Canadian: P.O. Box 609, Fort Erie, Ont. L2A 5X3

PROMOTED— TO WIFE!

Raye Morgan

Silhouette
ROMANCE™
Published by Silhouette Books
America's Publisher of Contemporary Romance

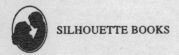

SILHOUETTE BOOKS

ISBN 0-373-19451-X

PROMOTED—TO WIFE!

Copyright © 2000 by Helen Conrad

This edition published by arrangement with Harlequin Books S.A.

Visit Silhouette at www.eHarlequin.com

Printed in U.S.A.

RAYE MORGAN

has spent almost two decades, while writing over fifty novels, searching for the answer to that elusive question: just what is that special magic that happens when a man and a woman fall in love? Every time she thinks she has the answer, a new wrinkle pops up, necessitating another book! Meanwhile, after living in Holland, Guam, Japan and Washington, D.C., she currently makes her home in Southern California with her husband and two of her four boys.

IT'S OUR 20th ANNIVERSARY!
We'll be celebrating all year,
Continuing with these fabulous titles,
On sale in June 2000.

CHAPTER TO WED

Chapter One

Kyra Symington watched as her spoon sank slowly into the hot fudge sundae, down into the soft whipped cream, sliding through the thick, deep chocolate, crunching into the buttery ice cream, curving and coming back with a load of the most delicious substances known to man. The diet was over. She'd lost twelve pounds, won the competition against her co-workers, and she was celebrating.

"You're going to gain it all right back," Chareen Wolf warned, pushing her straight silver-blond hair back behind her ears and watching her with envy. She and three other young women sat at a table in the employees' cafeteria and watched their honey-blond, brown-eyed co-worker eat, getting vicarious pleasure out of the fact that one of them was eating something besides the Confetti Caravel Cole Slaw of the Month. They'd all been on the diet. Chareen had lost eight pounds. Redheaded Gayle Smith had gained three. The others hadn't changed at all. There was no doubt about it. Kyra was the winner, and she deserved the ice cream. But Chareen couldn't resist another dig. "There must be a thousand calories in that thing."

"I know," Kyra said dreamily, gazing at the spoonful. The whipped cream was snow white, the ice cream pale golden, the fudge a rich liquid chocolate. Half the joy, she decided, was the anticipation. But the rest, she added to herself as the rich hot-and-cold sensations slipped into her mouth, was the tasting. It was nice to know that there were some things in life that didn't let you down. She looked around at the three faces watching her every move and she couldn't help but lay it on a little thicker.

"Mmm," she said, savoring the creamy flavors. Her friends were looking suitably jealous. She closed her eyes and let her head fall back, her golden-blond hair spilling behind her like a wavy river. "Ooh," she sighed, exaggerating the ecstasy just a bit, playing this for all it was worth. "Aaa." They were laughing at her by now. Slowly, she raised her head and opened her eyes, ready to laugh along with them, and found herself staring across the room, right into the bright turquoise gaze of the new director of Special Projects who was standing in the doorway, looking in. From the expression on his face, he'd heard every moan, watched every writhing moment of her faux ecstasy. And his crooked smile said he was enjoying it.

"Oh!" she said, gulping and looking quickly away.

The others watched this interchange in shock, then degenerated into snickers as Mr. Redman turned to greet a couple of his colleagues and left for the executive dining room.

"Oh my God, oh my God, oh my God!" Chareen muffled her shriek into her hands. "Did you see his face? Did you see that look?"

The others were just as deliciously scandalized.

Only Kyra sat silently, her face as red as her lunch tray. *I wish I could die,* she thought. *I wish I'd never been born. I wish King Kong would reach through the window and grab me. I wish...*

"Just wait. She'll get a raise."

"Or a promotion."

"Or Mr. Redman will ask her to come be his personal assistant."

"Hey, cutie," Gayle teased in a phony male voice. "Come help me work this copy machine."

"I'd help him work anything he was having trouble with," Chareen intoned suggestively, flipping her silky silver hair back over her shoulder and striking a pose. "I could even make a few recommendations myself."

The voices were swirling around her but Kyra hardly heard them. She was embarrassed, but that didn't mean she wasn't intrigued. She'd seen Mr. Redman from afar since he'd transferred from the Dallas branch office a few weeks earlier, and she'd had fleeting thoughts about his tall, hunky good looks. You couldn't miss the man. When he walked down the hall, there was a subtle fluttering, like wind through a wheat field, that followed in his wake— the fluttering, it seemed, of female attention. She'd noticed him all right. But what she'd just shared with him had stunned her. When she'd met his gaze, she had recognized something dancing behind his smile. Something had clicked.

At least on her part. She gave a little shiver and sighed. He probably didn't notice a thing. Why would he? Every woman on the eighth floor had gone gaga over the man. Women had to be a dime a dozen to him. He'd only been laughing at her little act. Laughing at *her*. Ugh. That wasn't fun to contemplate. She made a face and tuned back in to the conversation going on around her.

"Cheryl Pervis said he came on to her big time when she went in to help collate the Roberts report," Gayle was saying.

"Who? Mr. Redman?" Kyra asked, trying not to show her disappointment.

"Oh, Cheryl thinks the janitor is coming on to her when he asks her to move her legs so he can get the wastebasket out from under her desk," Chareen said caustically.

"Maybe," Gayle said doubtfully, her green eyes flashing. "But the man's a hound dog. Did you check out that smile? He's a player, ladies. That much is obvious."

Kyra tuned out again. She stared at her uneaten hot fudge sundae. It was starting to melt. How appropriate. *Sort of like my life,* she thought with a mental shrug. It would be fun to think the man had actually been attracted to her. It would certainly spice up the long hours around here. But things like that never seemed to happen to her these days. Men went for the flirty types, like Chareen, or the elegant ones, like Gayle. She'd just about decided men thought she was too serious. And maybe they were right.

It hadn't always been that way. She'd dated a lot

in high school. She'd never been one of the really popular girls, but she'd run around with a group of friends and they had all had a lot of fun together—dances and picnics and cruising to Catalina. By the end of her senior year, she'd thought she was in love.

Gary had been exciting and affectionate and she'd been so happy to find a man of her own, she hadn't noticed that everything they did revolved around him, not her. They had gone off to the same college and that had been fun, too. She really had to admit, even today, that having him with her had made a lot of things easier at the time.

But that all seemed a lifetime ago. Her parents had been killed in the crash of her father's light plane during her second semester in college, and nothing had been the same since. Her world had come crashing down around her shoulders. Not only had she had the horrifying grief of losing her parents, she'd come home to find her father's financial affairs in a shambles. Debts outweighed funds, and what little insurance they had had proved flimsy at best.

To make matters worse, Gary had faded into the woodwork. He certainly had no interest in getting involved in anything that wasn't entertaining. When the going got tough, he disappeared. She'd had a quick lesson in the futility of depending on a boyfriend when the chips were down.

Luckily, she'd had her grandparents to turn to. Her mother's parents didn't have much money, but they had plenty of love to shower on her, and she'd moved home to be with them, transferring to the local junior college and getting a job to help pay her expenses—not to mention making a start on clearing up what remained of her father's debts. Luckily, the job had been here at TriTerraCorp, a large real-estate development firm with ongoing projects all over the country. They specialized in resorts along the California coast and in Texas and Florida. The pay wasn't spectacular, but the four-story building was state-of-the-art, all tinted glass and brushed steel, with carpeted hallways and more individual offices rather than the cubicles prevalent in so many companies. It was a nice place to work in every day. But her work there, along with a second job she'd felt she had to take on, left little time for finding men to flirt with.

"Well, let us know if Mr. Redman invites you into the supply room for a private consultation," Chareen was saying, flashing Kyra a teasing look. "It's been so long since I've had any male attention, I'll get a thrill just hearing about his technique."

"You don't need male attention," Gayle shot back at her. "You've got those two little redheaded boys at home. You're one of the lucky ones."

Kyra glanced at Gayle, hearing the longing in her voice. The tall, beautiful woman had been trying to get pregnant for as long as she'd known her, but her husband was much older and in failing health, and so far, nothing—including a few fertility clinics—had helped. She would have given anything for a child.

And at the same time, Chareen, who had twins, didn't have a husband to go with them. She was having a tough time raising those two little mischievous boys on her own. Kyra suddenly felt ashamed of herself for complaining about her own life, even if silently. There were others who had more problems than she did. What right did she have to feel sorry for herself?

Lunch was over. She left most of her hot fudge sundae behind in the glass, despite the teasing she got from the other women. Her appetite seemed to have evaporated.

She caught sight of Mr. Redman as she came out of the cafeteria. He was heading in the opposite direction with a group of men and he didn't notice her, but her heart did a little cartwheel as she noted his wide shoulders and she couldn't suppress a giggle. How silly was that! *You'd think I was a teenage girl,* she scolded herself, and vowed not to let that happen again—at least not where anyone could see her behaving like a ninny.

She went back to her desk and got to work on client correspondence. She had a pile of letters that needed answering and she had to get out on time that night. Her second job started at six and she would just have time to stop by home and make sure her grandmother was okay before going to the restaurant. Eight hours at TriTerraCorp and another four hours at the Rusty Scupper made for a long day.

And it certainly left no time to daydream about the new director of Special Projects, even if he was the sexiest man in the building these days.

She sighed and stopped what she was doing for a moment to indulge in a little daydreaming anyway. It didn't get you into trouble like real dating did. She could dream about him and never have to say she was sorry!

And he was a great subject for daydreams. Mr. Redman. She wondered what his first name was. Most of the executives were paunchy and balding

—not to mention married. But Mr. Redman was as young and handsome as a film star, and he had a casual, crooked grin that sent hearts fluttering on a daily basis.

He also had rumors flying around the offices. They said he was a heartbreaker. They said he was a flirt. And yet, no one could name anyone who had actually gone out with him. No one had actually seen him on the town. And that only added to the speculation and the interest. What was the man all about, anyway?

Kyra couldn't get him out of her mind that evening as she showed parties to their tables at the Rusty Scupper. She'd worked as hostess there for almost a year and she'd never seen him come in. But a lot of the executives from TriTerraCorp did patronize the restaurant and that night she kept expecting to see him every time she turned around to greet a new couple entering the restaurant. She wasn't sure why that was. Wishful thinking, maybe. But if he did appear, surely he would have a woman on his arm. So what was she expecting? Better she should forget those turquoise eyes and focus on her job.

And the next day, when she went back to work at TriTerraCorp, she glanced toward his office as she got off the elevator, then looked away quickly, scolding herself for foolishness. She was going to have to stop this. She was becoming obsessed and there was absolutely no reason for it.

She spent the morning creating a set of spreadsheets on her computer and almost decided to skip lunch because she was so busy. She had just made a mistake on a column of figures and was going to have to start all over again, so she wasn't very receptive when Chareen stopped by her desk.

"Coming to lunch?" her silver-haired friend asked.

Kyra made a face. "I don't know. I might just grab a candy bar and—"

"No you don't. You didn't spend all this time dieting just to go back to old habits." Chareen stood over her desk tapping her foot impatiently. "Come on. You can spare a few minutes to have a bite of something better for you than a candy bar. You probably need a break anyway. You'll come back rested and ready to tackle things with a fresh outlook."

Kyra smiled at her personal philosopher. "You know something? For once, you've said something sensible. You're absolutely right." She grabbed her purse and rose to join her. "Let's go."

They went through the cafeteria line, filled their trays and met the others at their usual table. The room was cheerfully decorated with several tables clustered around an open pit fireplace. In the winter the fireplace was lit, and in the summer it was filled with ferns and pots of pink and white cyclamens. They ate quickly, chattering about inconsequential items as they went. It was good, Kyra thought, to be with friends and relax for a few minutes. Catching a warm smile from Gayle and watching Chareen's huge eyes flash as she let loose one of her zingers reminded her that these were moments she cherished. Friends. She loved them all. Who needed a man in her life?

And suddenly, there he was again. They all fell silent as he appeared in the doorway, and this time he came into the large, high-ceilinged room that offered a variety of meals to employees—and he was coming right toward them! He looked as good as ever, his suit crisp and expensive-looking, his eyes an incredible shade of sea blue-green. There was something about the man—even when he was across the room, Kyra imagined that she could smell his aftershave and sense the heat lying in wait under that crisp white shirt.

The women all stared as he strode confidently their way, stopping right at their table and looking at each one of them in turn.

"Hello, ladies," he said, glancing around the room and then back at them. "I thought I would stop by and take a look at the employee cafeteria. I've never really been in here before."

Chareen found her voice first. "Well, here it is," she said cheekily. "Right where you'd expect it to be."

He smiled at her. "Yes, isn't it?" He shared his smile with the rest of them. "My name is James Redman. And you are…?"

He was looking at Chareen, so she introduced herself and the others followed suit around the table.

"Tracy Martin."

"Gayle Smith."

"Ann Marie Hope."

"Kyra Symington." She was the last and he looked at her the longest, repeating her name softly to himself. There was an awkward pause and she felt as though something else was needed to fill it, so she stuck out her hand. He shook hands with her, then held on a moment longer than was necessary, repeating her name once more as though he was memorizing it.

Her pulse began to race. What on earth was the man up to? She tugged on her hand and he let it go, but he was smiling at her.

"What have you got there?" he asked, looking down at her plate. "A Caesar salad?"

"Yes."

"How is it?"

"It's…quite good, thanks." His smile was curling her toes. "Would you like a bite?" she asked without thinking.

They stared at each other for a beat too long. Muffled gasps and stifled giggles could be heard around the table and she wanted to have a few friends executed as soon as possible. Or at least banished to a distant kingdom. This was crazy, surreal, and she didn't have a clue why it was happening.

"Not right now, thanks," he said at last, his brilliant gaze caressing her in a sensuous way that stopped her heart in her throat. "Maybe I'll take a rain check on it."

Smiling at them all, he turned and sauntered toward the doorway, looking for all the world like a young god leaving the plebian realm and heading for the loftier atmosphere of the executive dining room.

"That didn't just happen, did it?" Chareen could hardly contain herself. "I was dreaming, right?" Kyra stifled a silent scream. "Did you see the way he looked at you? Did you get those double entendres?"

Kyra felt robotic, moving jerkily, automatically. "I don't think he meant anything at all," she said stiffly, stabbing at her salad with her fork.

"You are blind! He meant a lot, babe. His eyes were speaking volumes."

"Ooh, Kyra," Ann Marie said, her silky black hair falling over one violet eye. "He's got a thing for you. That's obvious!"

Kyra shook her head. "No, no, I'm sure…"

"Ten to one he'll call you into his office this afternoon."

"Just watch out," Chareen crowed. "If he calls you into his office, better take your pepper spray!"

"Forget the pepper spray," Gayle purred. "Take your negligee."

Chareen laughed. "Okay, I'm taking bets. I bet he tries to kiss her."

Gayle snorted. "I say he throws her down on top of the desk and makes mad passionate love to her."

"Ouch!" Ann Marie chimed in. "She'll end up with pencils stuck in her back. I say he opts for the carpet. I hear it's pretty thick in his office."

Quiet Tracy looked around the table, listening to each in turn, then said softly, "*I* think he'll ask her out on a date."

They all turned to look at her. Sweet and younger than the rest, she always had an outlook that stopped the more cynical among them in their tracks. They all stared at her for a moment, mulling over what she'd said.

But Chareen would have none of it once she'd thought it over. "No way. Executives don't ask office workers out on dates. It isn't done."

Tracy lifted her chin. "Well then, why would she want to have anything to do with him?"

Kyra smiled at her. A voice of sanity. She welcomed it. "You're right. Why would I?"

There were groans all around, but Kyra held her ground. Tracy was on the money. Either things were done the correct way, or they shouldn't be done at all. She put down her fork, bundled together the remains of her meal and stood.

"Remember that song? 'R-E-S-P-E-C-T.'" She gave a snap of her fingers and started sashaying toward the trash barrel, still singing. Her friends were laughing and at the door, she gave them a little bow and left, still smiling.

But the smile was gone before she was back at her desk and staring into her computer monitor. The spreadsheet was still in trouble and there was a stack of new work in her in-box. No time to think about bosses with sexy smiles. She had to get these things done. She wanted to leave early that day. She had to get a prescription filled for her grandmother, and Nurse O'Brien, who stayed with her in the afternoons, had asked her to pick up some medicated hand lotion while she was at the drugstore. Work was always there, always piling higher, always looking more and more insurmountable.

"Stiff upper lip," she told herself softly. "Nose to the grindstone. A penny saved is a penny earned." Or something like that. Whatever. Work. That was the thing. And she knew how to get things done, so she might as well get to it.

Chareen stopped by an hour later on her way to the copy machine. Kyra was finally getting the spreadsheet squared away.

"Any messages from Mr. Wonderful yet?" Chareen asked in a stage whisper.

Kyra flashed her a baleful look. "Messages, smessages. I've got work to do, lady."

Chareen raised a painted eyebrow. "You know what they say. All work and no play…"

"Allows me to draw a paycheck. Will you get out of here? I am so far behind."

Chareen left, but the thought she'd planted lingered after her and began to bedevil Kyra. Mr. Redman couldn't possibly have any interest in her—but he really had held her hand too long. And repeated her name twice. And he really had given her a smile like he had given no one else at the table. Did that mean anything?

But so what if it did? Was she crazy? She wasn't going to respond to any sort of pass from a playboy. Chareen had been right. Executives didn't seriously date office workers. And if they showed interest, they had only one thing on their minds. What she'd said at lunch had been true. A woman needed to respect herself. She'd never been anyone's plaything and she never would be. She was serious, a woman who had been forced to work hard for a long time just to keep her head above water. She certainly didn't have time to waste on frivolous fantasies about the boss.

And yet, he *had* held her hand too long….

Lost in thought, she didn't notice her supervisor approaching until she'd stopped at her desk.

"What have you been up to?" the older woman asked, her lips pursed and her eyes cool. "I didn't know you were interested in transferring to Special Projects."

"What?" Kyra looked at Alice Beals, blinking. "I haven't asked for a transfer."

"Really?" Alice looked skeptical. "Then why is the new Special Projects director asking questions about your availability?"

Color flooded her cheeks and she felt the room

spin for a quick succession of seconds. "I...that is...he...what? Do you mean Mr. Redman?"

"If there's anyone else heading up Special Projects at the moment, I haven't heard about it."

"No. I mean..."

"Yes, Mr. Redman. His secretary just called asking if you could be spared for some sort of public relations project they are developing."

Her heart was thumping in her chest. This was unreal. "What did you say?"

She shrugged. "Directors of departments get what they want. I said you would be happy to drop everything and run right over, ruining all my schedules and leaving us with a huge hole in our workforce." She looked about ready to tear her hair out, but then her eyes narrowed and she gazed beyond Kyra. "I know. I can play this game, too. I'll ask Finance to loan me Sharon Nishiyama to take your place. I'll say Mr. Hoover requested her." Her eyes gleamed with satisfaction as she turned away, her thoughts already engaged in new manipulations.

"Alice," Kyra called after her. "What am I supposed to do?"

Alice looked back and snorted. "Your work, what else? She only asked about your availability. She said she'd get back to us."

"Oh."

Kyra took a deep breath and steadied herself. There was no point in trying to analyze what was going on, because this was all so different from what she was used to. She'd worked there for two years and nothing like this had ever happened to her before. The best thing to do was exactly what Alice had advised—her work. She forced herself to stare at her computer monitor, but nothing seemed to register with her brain, and she was almost relieved when a young woman appeared at her desk and asked, "Are you Kyra Symington?"

Kyra looked up and paused. She recognized her right away—it was Pam Haines, Mr. Redman's administrative assistant. Her heart began to thump faster again, and yet by then there was a feeling of inevitability to it all.

"Yes, I'm Kyra," she said, unconsciously sitting a little straighter and lifting her chin.

"Mr. Redman would like to see you in his office. He asked that you appear at four o'clock. He has something he wants to talk to you about."

"Four o'clock?" she repeated. "Uh, I guess that will be all right." She was planning to leave at four-thirty. Maybe she should tell the administrative assistant....

But the young woman was already gone, and now Kyra had something new to worry about. What on earth could he want? Chareen's and Gayle's jokes about him coming on to her kept bobbing around in her mind. She told herself their theories were ridiculous, but she couldn't blot them out. The way he'd smiled at her! Her mouth went dry at the memory of it.

Then there was another worry. Would it take longer than half an hour? Would she annoy him if she said she couldn't hang around this evening to learn more about this mysterious project? On the other hand, staying after-hours with a man like that would be asking for trouble. Was she going to have to be ready to defend herself against aggressive flirting?

Actually, she thought to herself as she put files away and cleared her desk, she rather doubted that. He probably wanted her opinion on the cafeteria food. Or he'd decided she might like to take charge of a program of entertainment for the employees' picnic. Or he needed someone to stuff envelopes on the weekends. Oh, who knew what he wanted? Whatever it was all about, he'd ruined her concentration for the rest of the day, and she found herself in the lounge, studying herself in the mirror and reaching for her makeup bag.

Even as she freshened her mascara and pulled the comb through her hair, she wondered what on earth she thought she was doing. She was worried he might try to come on to her, so she was busily attempting to make herself more attractive. Did that make any sense? Of course not. She pulled the zipper on her makeup bag and stuffed it back in her purse, giving herself a dirty look in the mirror. Enough of that.

But even though she went back to her desk she couldn't get any work done. She went over her options in her mind. The way she saw it, there were only two possibilities. Either he would ask her to do something legitimate and business-like that she would either agree to do or refuse to do—or he would attempt to entice her into a romantic situation. The more she thought about it, the more she tended to discount the last possibility. The man had his pick of the place. Why would he choose her?

Chapter Two

James Redman balanced a pencil on the edge of an eraser and watched it totter until it lost its stability and fell to the surface of the cherry-wood desk. Then he allowed himself a few moments to think about his life.

He loved his job. He worked hard, and he had been working even harder than usual lately, finding a place for himself in the West Coast branch office of TriTerraCorp. He'd been brought in from Texas to take over Contract Negotiations, but there had been a snafu and he'd been handed Special Projects on an interim basis while they were getting things cleared up. He was bound and determined to prove himself there in the meantime, and that took hard work.

In his time he had been known to play pretty hard, too. But not lately. Ever since his thirtieth birthday, his appetite for play had gone downhill.

"It's only natural," his Aunt Jo had told him when he'd complained to her about it a few months earlier.

"It's time for you to get married. To everything there is a season, and your matrimonial cycle is due to arrive, like an oncoming train. You can't avoid it."

He shuddered as he remembered her words. The woman was a menace. Too bad he loved her like a son. But there were some things he wouldn't do, even for love, and marriage was one of them.

A signal chimed softly on his control board and he frowned at it. He still hadn't learned to interpret the chimes, buzzes and flashing lights on the thing. It was usually safest to check with his secretary before answering anything. He clicked to her station.

"What is it, Pam?" he asked her.

"The call is on line one. I believe the young lady said her name was—" Pam cleared her throat in a decorous manner "—Piccadilly, sir. That's what it sounded like."

"Piccadilly?" He grinned. "Oh, you mean Pica Delay. Her accent can throw you off. She's an old friend. Put her through."

Pam hesitated. "Mr. Redman, I believe I've explained to you. All you have to do is press the button on your—"

"Oh, right," he said quickly. "I forgot. Thanks, Pam." He swore softly as he punched buttons. The system in Dallas had been installed around the time Lincoln was shot. He was used to a secretary who did everything for him, including greeting him with coffee already poured the way he liked it when he came in mornings. The setup here in California was supposed to be the latest thing going. So how come he ended up doing so much more of the work this way?

"Pica?" he said into the receiver. "Is that really you?"

The high-pitched shriek on the other end of the line suggested an answer in the affirmative. "Jamie darling! I have found you at last! I've been hunting up and down this coast for days. Why didn't you tell me Rio de Oro was a real town? I was looking for a resort and—"

"Yes, well, you're here now," he said hurriedly, heading off the launch into explanation overkill she was obviously prepared to embark upon. "Where are you staying?"

She heaved a sensuous sigh, made for effect. "Well, darling. I was hoping—"

"Can't do it, Pica. My aunt is in and out of my apartment. And anyway, I'm working my tail off these days. I wouldn't have time to treat you like a guest. You'd better check into the Hilton. I'll pick up the tab." The thing about his aunt was a fib. She did stay at his apartment occasionally, but at the moment, she was in Egypt. She wasn't likely to drop in from there. But you couldn't be too careful. He'd learned to avoid letting any woman think she might have a chance of taking over his life.

"Whatever you say, Jamie," Pica said with a sigh. "I'm just so anxious to see you!"

"Me, too. How about dinner? I'll come by your hotel at seven. Okay?"

"Of course. We'll eat in." She gave him a few little noisy kisses. "I'll go right up and take a long, refreshing bath so that we can—"

"Right," he said quickly, suddenly wondering if Pam ever listened in to his phone conversations. "'Til then."

"Mmm, hmm. It's been so long since we—"

"Hasn't it though? Gotta go." He plunked down the phone and took a deep breath. Well. Pica was in town. Good thing. He flexed his shoulders and thought about her hourglass figure with a smile. He could use a little relaxation. He hadn't had a real date since…

"Mr. Redman."

He looked up as Pam Haines entered carrying an armload of files. "Did you want to look over these other personnel files?"

That reminded him—he had a few things he needed to take care of. He was in the midst of planning a series of promotional events and he had developed a scheme that had gone over big with the CEO. His idea included creating a special unit of employees to act as elite assistants to the project. He wanted to assemble that unit right away.

"Fine," he told his secretary as she showed him the files. "Just put them here on my desk. I want to go through them all this afternoon."

She dumped them and looked at him. "You don't want any help? I know a lot of the employees pretty well. I could probably—"

"No thanks, Pam," he said. "Not at this point, anyway. I'm just developing my criteria as I go along. Playing it by ear. When I get a better idea of what I'm looking for, I may ask for your help." He glanced her way. "You did tell the Symington woman I wanted to see her?"

"Yes. She'll be here at four." She looked at her watch. "I'll show her in, and then I'm going to take off. Geoffrey is flying in from New York and I told him I would meet him at the airport. You don't mind, do you?''

He barely glanced at her in his absentmindedness. "Mmm? Oh, no, of course not. Say hello to your wandering husband for me, Pam. And I'll see you first thing tomorrow.''

He stared at the stack of files as she left the room. He was considering offering the first job on his team to Kyra Symington. For some reason, she fit the image he'd created this idea around. And anyway, she seemed a nice young woman and she'd been recommended by her department head. Besides, something about her appealed to him. He glanced at his slim and very expensive gold watch—a gift from his Aunt Jo on his last birthday—to see how punctual Miss Symington was.

"Come in," he called when the knock came at his door right at four.

He watched Kyra walk into his office and frowned, studying her with objective dispassion. He wasn't really sure. There were a number of elements in her favor. For one thing, she looked terrific. Her face was pretty in a serene way he liked. Her body was trim, her breasts nicely prominent and her bearing graceful. She didn't wear the tight, short skirts and skimpy tops the women in the offices seemed to favor these days, and that was a plus. Not that he had anything against sexy clothes. He just didn't want someone wearing that sort of thing on his team. No, she didn't dress like a teenager. At the same time, she was hardly frumpy. Classic lines—that was what she had. Just the sort of woman he would choose—for whatever.

The only thing that didn't seem to fit her otherwise

quiet style was her hair. She wore it loose and free rather than folding it into a French twist or tying it back. Honey-blond with golden accents that caught the light, it spilled in luscious waves around her face and down her back. He couldn't keep his gaze off it. He'd wanted to touch it from the first time he'd noticed her, sink his fingers into the richness of it and…

But that was neither here nor there. The point was, she fit the bill physically.

And her résumé was fine, full of evidence of a certain dignified sense of responsibility that he liked. He didn't need a party girl in this role. What he wanted was a woman who was stable and mature, yet captivating enough to be appealing to clients. She would be meeting with potential investors, escorting them to projected development sites, painting pictures in their heads of what could be and how very much they were going to want to be a part of it all. She would be representing TriTerraCorp—be the public face of the company. She was twenty-six, just the right age. She should be well over silly schoolgirl emotions. On the whole, she seemed to be just about perfect.

Perfect. Just the sort of woman a man like him might… An idea hit him like a brick to the head and he almost gasped aloud. A conversation he'd had with his aunt came back to him and this bolt from the blue seemed like an answer to a problem that had been haunting him ever since. Kyra Symington was, in some ways, the image of his ideal woman. If she bore out her image, she would be able to help him a lot with his work. And maybe with a problem in his personal life, too.

But no. It was just too crazy. Mentally, he shook

himself. He had to put that away. He couldn't think about it now. He had to conduct an interview with this perfect specimen who looked so good on paper.

Now to see if she could match up in the flesh— so to speak.

"We meet again," he said, rising to shake hands with her and offer her a seat. "I enjoyed our visit in the cafeteria today."

She murmured something polite as she sank into the chair and tried to see behind his rather formal smile. She was nervous, but only in a wary sort of way, because she just didn't get it. In the cafeteria he'd been all bedroom eyes—but right now, he seemed all business. Her fingers curled around the notebook she'd brought along in the event she needed to take notes. Or in case she needed a weapon.

Still, she had to admit the man was overwhelmingly attractive. His dark hair was slightly rumpled, as though he'd been running his fingers through it in exasperation over some knotty dilemma he was working on. But his suit was impeccable, his white shirt crisp against skin that looked warmly tanned. And his eyelashes…he had the longest eyelashes she'd ever seen on a man, long, thick and silky black, framing those brilliant sea-blue eyes in a way that set them off even more spectacularly. She felt her pulse begin to race. The man was dangerously sexy.

"Do you enjoy working here at TriTerraCorp, Miss Symington?" he asked smoothly, sitting casually on the corner of the desk and looking down at her.

"Very much," she said, figuring a white lie that saved her job was worth it.

"Have you had any thoughts of doing something else with your life?"

She stared up at him, blinking. "I'd like to complete my college degree someday," she said slowly. "But other than that…"

"How about marriage?"

She stiffened, surprised by the question. This was really weird. He wasn't flirting at all, and yet he was asking questions so personal, she felt like snapping at him. Where had that provocative man from lunch gone, anyway? "What *about* marriage?" she said, her chin up and her tone just short of challenging.

His turquoise eyes seemed to bore into her, seeing things she would rather no one knew about. "Do you have any plans along those lines? Are you engaged to anyone?"

This was none of his business, was it? She wasn't sure, but she thought she'd heard they weren't allowed to ask you questions like this anymore. "What does that have to do with my job?" she asked, and this time the challenge was unmistakable.

Something shifted behind his sea-blue eyes and she realized, suddenly, that she'd somehow hit a nerve. He nodded, watching her, his gaze running over her hair, her collarbone, her breasts, the knees she couldn't quite cover though she'd tugged on the hem of her dress. She had the uneasy feeling she was being graded somehow. He didn't say anything, and she waited. It was becoming evident that he hadn't called her in to make a play for her after all. If he had, and this was his version of flirting, the man didn't deserve his reputation. She waited. His eyes narrowed as he looked her over, and the hair on the back of her neck began to tingle. What was he up to?

"No serious boyfriend?" he asked at last.

Her head jerked back and her dark eyes flashed. "Mr. Redman, these are very odd questions. I don't understand…" She began to rise from her chair and he stepped forward to stop her.

"Stay, Kyra. Please. There is a method to this, believe me. I'm not just fishing for personal information for the fun of it." He tried a smile but it didn't quite reach his eyes. "I have my reasons for asking. I need to be clear on your availability to work long hours, evenings, weekends, etc. But we'll…uh…let that go for now."

She hesitated. She wasn't sure she trusted him, but when she looked into his eyes again, something she saw there convinced her to give him a chance, and she sank back into the chair.

He walked around the desk and sat in his own chair, and when he met her gaze again, something had changed in his eyes, as though he'd come to a decision about something, and he smiled at her—a cool, detached smile, but a better smile than the last one.

"I have taken the liberty of looking over your personnel file," he said. "I wanted to find out everything I could about you for a very specific reason." He leaned forward and gazed directly into her eyes. "I have a special job coming up and I'm looking for someone to fill it. In fact, I'd like to hire you for the position."

She froze, wary to the tips of her toes. This wasn't the way these things were usually done. But she had to admit, the thought of working for him was certainly intriguing.

He stood and began to pace the office. She watched him, suspended in anticipation, but even so, she couldn't avoid noticing the muscular outline of his thighs beneath the light woolen slacks. And a tiny part of her gave a whimper of regret that he hadn't brought her up there to make a pass. She hadn't been the recipient of many passes in her time. She could have used one right about now.

"I don't know if Pam told you anything about the position I'm preparing to offer you."

She shook her head. "I'm afraid I don't know what you're talking about."

He frowned and shoved his hands deep into the pockets of his slacks. "You have heard of the Black Stone Beach Resort development?"

Black Stone Beach was going to be a stunning destination resort just south of Carmel and Monterey along the California coast. Three golf courses were planned, along with a walk-through aquarium in the ocean, an ice rink, three Olympic-size swimming pools, and a hotel with a waterfall in every room.

"Oh, yes. They say it will be the biggest job we've ever worked on."

He nodded. "That's right. In time, it will probably consume most of our resources here in Rio de Oro. Every department will be expected to clear the decks to make room for it. But right now, only a few have been assigned to it. What I am suggesting will be one of those assignments."

He continued pacing, but as he walked, he explained to her about the team he wanted to put together to host promotional events, going over his hopes for the project, making it sound very exciting.

"Potential investors will be coming in from all over the country," he told her. "We'll be arranging bus trips to visit Hearst Castle, a beach party with a bonfire, a limousine caravan to the opera in Santa Barbara. We'll need at least three assistants to help make arrangements and to host the clients during the events." He stopped before her and looked down into her eyes. "And I'd like you to administer the team."

"Me?" She hoped her voice wasn't really as squeaky as it sounded in her own ears. To say she was shocked would have been an understatement.

He nodded. "You'll be on short-term loan from your department. I'm requesting you for a six-month stint at this point, with an option to extend if things work out as I hope they will. What do you say?"

What did she say? This was the sort of thing she'd dreamed about for years—a job with something more interesting to do than type and file and make phone calls asking for bank balances. He hadn't said anything about more money, but even if it didn't pay much more, it would help give her the experience she needed to ask for a promotion later on. And best of all, it sounded like fun! The only problem was...

She sighed. "I'm sorry, Mr. Redman. I'm afraid I won't be able to accept your offer." It made her want to cry from sheer frustration.

A frown darkened his face. He wasn't pleased and the hard edge to his voice revealed it. "May I ask why not?"

"Sure." She gazed into his eyes with candid regret. "I've got another job. I'm not available evenings at all, and only every other weekend."

He stared. "Another job? Where? Doing what?"

"I'm a hostess at the Rusty Scupper, down on Devega Street."

He glared at her as though she'd admitted she worked in a strip club. "What are you, a single mother?"

She flushed. "No. I have my reasons." Realizing that sounded a bit defensive, she added, "I have some bills that have to be taken care of. I have no choice."

"Even if I managed to engineer a raise for you?"

That gave her pause, but she knew it was no use. He wouldn't be able to squeeze enough money out of the top management to make it worth her while to quit her extra job. Besides, after six months, she'd be out pounding the pavement again, looking for another moonlighter. No, tempting as it was to think of working with this dazzling man, she couldn't do it.

"I'm sorry, Mr. Redman. It's impossible."

He stared at her for a long moment, his gaze lingering on her hair. "Nothing is impossible," he told her shortly. Without giving her time to answer, he began to pace again, telling her more about his plans for the project as if she hadn't answered yet and just needed more convincing. He wasn't used to being turned down by women. He had a feeling if he could just make her see how well planned this was, she would change her mind and beg to be included.

But it wasn't working. She wasn't even turning to watch him pace any longer. She was just sitting there, staring down at her hands. And her hair, that magnificent sweep of silk, was tumbling down her back. It was the most gorgeous hair he'd ever noticed before. He itched to touch it. He was coming closer and closer. All he had to do was reach out as he passed....

"Don't close your mind to this yet," he said as he came up behind her. "Think it over for a day or so." Another step, and he would be right behind her. His hand seemed to move toward her hair of its own accord. "I really want you as part of our team." There. He'd done it, his fingertips barely grazing the tendrils. It felt like the fur on a baby kitten, so soft, so ethereal. He wanted to grab a handful of it and bring it to his face.... But she'd noticed he'd stopped moving and when she turned her head and saw how close he was, she was startled and jumped out of her seat, catching him by surprise. He jerked away, but not fast enough. Somehow her hair got tangled in his watchband, and suddenly they were tied together.

"Ouch!" she cried, reaching up blindly to save her hair from being yanked.

"Hey," he said, stopping her with his free hand. "Wait a minute. We're caught here."

Caught was hardly the word for it. They were locked together, her face just inches from his hand.

"I'll get it," he said firmly. "Just hold still."

He bent close, working on freeing her hair. She held her breath, trying to blot out the sense of him, trying to avoid his scent. But it was no use. She could feel his warm breath tickling her cheek. Surely he could hear her heart beating as though she'd just run the mile.

"Breathe," he ordered brusquely. "I don't want you passing out in my office."

She let air in and looked up at him. He was frowning intently at the knot; but he turned his gaze to meet hers and gave her a lopsided grin. "You see?" he said softly, his eyes smoky with some emotion she didn't want to name. "We belong together. You have to come work for me."

By the end of his comment, his smile was fading and his gaze had shifted to her mouth. His fingers paused as he stared at her lips and a strange look of hunger filled his blue-green eyes. Her heart was pounding so hard, it was like a drum beating in her head. Was he going to kiss her? Oh please, please... Her lips parted. She didn't think she'd ever wanted anything so intensely before in her life. She closed her eyes, as if that would give them both cover. And she swayed toward him, aching for the touch of his lips on hers.

"There," he said suddenly, and she felt him drawing away. "Sorry about that. I hope I didn't hurt you."

She opened her eyes with a start, blinking at him as he walked briskly back to slump in the chair behind his desk.

"Now if you'll excuse me, Miss Symington, I have a lot of work to do." He was pulling out files, his attention completely diverted. He looked as though he hardly remembered why he'd asked her to his office. "I'll have my secretary type up a formal offer and have it ready for you in the morning. Let me know by...oh, say ten o'clock Friday morning. Thank you for coming in."

He didn't look up. After a few seconds of pure shock, she turned blindly toward the door. She'd been dismissed, just like that. He was finished with her.

Well, that was okay. She wanted to get as far away from this man as she could just as quickly as possible. The best destination would be a soundproof room where she could scream and throw pillows and call him a few four-letter names.

When would she ever learn? You couldn't count on a man. She'd given her heart to Gary, thought she was ready to commit for life, but the moment trouble had come her way, he'd looked for greener pastures. No doubt about it, James Redman was a very similar type.

"What a jerk the man is!" she muttered as she made her way to the parking lot, late as usual. Mortified, she pictured him back at his desk, probably laughing his head off over the way he'd made her swoon. "I can give you your answer right now, Mr. Redman. I wouldn't work for you, not for anything! Not if I was starving. Not if you gave me the company and told me to do with it what I wanted. Not for anything!"

Not even if he had actually kissed her. But she couldn't help thinking about it.

Chapter Three

"Atmosphere," Duane Boyd, the manager of the Rusty Scupper always said. "That's the key to our success. Every one of us has to work to maintain the proper atmosphere. We don't want to ever send out a jarring note to our customers."

Luckily, Kyra thought as she took a deep breath and began to prepare mentally for the night ahead, *luckily Duane had also hired a top-notch chef.* Otherwise his beloved atmosphere wouldn't last long enough to keep a fern alive.

And ferns were central to his atmosphere. "We're a little piece of tropical paradise set down on the central California coast," he liked to say. The ferns helped. So did the fake waterfall in the entryway and the soft pseudo-Polynesian music with the muted birdcalls, meant to make you feel as though you'd just stepped into a rain forest hideaway. Not to mention the little umbrellas in the drinks.

For Kyra, it meant dressing in a sarong-style

sheath that flattered her curves and left one shoulder
bare. It was also the reason she'd grown accustomed
to wearing her hair loose. She had to on this job, and
she found she rather liked it that way. That night she
had it swept back behind one ear, a white gardenia
nestled in a bed of small waxy green leaves holding
her hair in place.

"It's going to be a corker tonight," Duane was
telling her and Shawna, the other hostess on this evening, rubbing his thick hands together in anticipation.
"We've got every banquet room sold out. The biggest is some band or musical group or something in
the Aloha Room. Birthday party. I've got Marge,
Lenny and Sharon on it. Hopefully, they'll be able
to handle things. But if they run into trouble and you
two get a free minute, you'll give them a hand, won't
you?"

"You can always count on me," Shawna sang out,
her shiny black hair swinging as she left to check
things in the kitchen.

"Of course," Kyra told him, going over the seating chart at the front desk and barely paying any
attention to him. Despite having already worked a
full day, she had plenty of energy left. She was used
to this.

Besides, her encounter with James Redman had
filled her with adrenaline that had to get used up
somehow. Some people went to the gym or their favorite neighborhood workout center to relieve stress.
She worked here. And tonight, she had stress to
spare. It still made her boil to think of the way he'd
teased her, then, once he'd begun to reel her in,
drawn back as though he hadn't meant a thing. She

felt herself clenching up every time she thought of it.

Besides, he'd made her late. She'd hurried to the pharmacy and rushed home. There'd been time to kiss her beloved grandmother's cheek and that was about all. Nurse O'Brien had wanted to talk to her, but she'd had no time for it. She had to carry on a conversation with the woman while she jumped on one foot, trying to pull off her office clothes and get into her sarong dress. The woman had been going on and on about a sister who was ill or something. She wasn't sure what. Her mind had still been too full of her anger at James Redman to make heads or tails of it. She felt a wave of guilt over her inattention and vowed to get the full story from her the next day.

At any rate, she got there only five minutes late, and that wasn't too bad when you came right down to it. The main dining room was almost half full already and the customers were beginning to arrive in steadily increasing numbers. The restaurant was popular and her working style was very different there than it was at TriTerraCorp. The pace accelerated to frantic levels and she often found herself moving on a strange, almost hypnotic plane where her actions flowed into each other and she reacted by instinct as much as by design. She was so into things by eight o'clock, she didn't even realize the new couple she was speaking to were Gayle and her much older husband until Gayle spoke and snapped her out of her trancelike state.

"Hey," Gayle said, laughing. "It's me. You can't have forgotten me since lunch."

Kyra did a double take and laughed along with

her. "Gayle! I'm sorry. I get so wrapped up in the pandemonium around here, I hardly remember my own name, much less anyone else's."

Gayle introduced her husband, Greg Smith. Kyra shook his hand, noticing with a twinge of anxiety that the man looked thin and rather pale. She knew he had health problems, and he certainly looked as though they were troubling him at the moment.

"I have to tell you a secret," Gayle said as Kyra started to lead them to their table. She bent close and spoke privately against the noise of the waterfall as they passed it. "We're celebrating. It finally took."

"Took?" Kyra gazed at her blankly, then remembered and realized what she was talking about. "Oh, your doctor's appointment. You're…oh Gayle! You're pregnant?"

Gayle nodded, smiling, and Kyra threw her arms around her friend and hugged her. "Oh, I'm so happy for you," she told her, truly delighted. "You *should* celebrate. This has been so long in coming!"

Gayle nodded again. "It has," she said. "And we are very happy." She gave Kyra a cautionary look. "Though it is early. There's no telling what might happen," she warned. "I don't want everyone to know just yet."

"Of course."

Kyra seated them beneath a bower of silk orchids, congratulating them both again, but as she turned away, she couldn't help but think that Gayle's husband, despite his ill health, looked a lot happier than she did. Somehow Gayle's joy seemed tinged with a certain sadness.

But she didn't have time to dwell on it. She ordered a special appetizer to be sent to their table as

a gift from her, then turned her attention back to her
duties. The musical people who had reserved the biggest banquet room were beginning to arrive. From
the looks of it, they were mostly accordion players
in bell-bottoms and puffy silk shirts. And from the
sound of it, they were going to be a noisy crew. She
glanced at her watch. It was only a little after eight.
Three hours to go.

James gave over his shiny black Porsche to the
valet and offered his arm to Pica. She took it gladly,
but it didn't make a dent in her running monologue
about some old friends they'd both known in Dallas.
He wasn't really listening. He was anticipating their
entrance into the restaurant and thinking about what
had happened earlier that afternoon.

Kyra Symington had surprised him. He thought he
knew women. After all, he'd been dating for years,
and he'd always been very careful not to get tied
down to just one person, so his experience had been
pretty extensive. He felt easy around women, casual,
sure of himself. It was a rare female who didn't suc-
cumb to his friendly approach, and he expected to be
attractive to any woman he was attracted to himself.
But something different had happened when he'd
caught his watchband in Kyra's hair. He'd looked
down into her eyes and he'd seen a response coming
from deep inside her, something visceral, something
she didn't seem to know how to control, and suddenly he'd been out of control himself, his body re-
acting to her as though he'd been a callow teenager
whose hormones were waging war against him. His
instinctive reaction had been to get away from her,

to sit down behind his desk and pretend that nothing was happening.

But something had happened, and he'd finally decided he knew what it was. They connected. They had some sort of spiritual bond. That was why he'd noticed her in the cafeteria the day before, and why he'd reacted to her the way he had. And that meant that she would be perfect for the role he wanted her to play in his life. He had to make her see that as well.

In the meantime, he had to put up with Pica. As they approached the desk, just avoiding a spray from the waterfall running slightly amok, she segued from describing Miss Minnie's case of shingles into exclaiming over the beauty of the tropic decor without seeming to feel any need to take a breath. James wondered, fleetingly, why he'd never noticed her unstoppable mouth before. He supposed it hadn't ever mattered. He had never dated her because of her sparkling wit or knowledgeable conversation. Her talking had always seemed like background noise before. Now, it was just annoying.

There was a hostess at the desk, but it wasn't Kyra. The woman was lovely, but she wasn't the one he was looking for. He glanced around the room surreptitiously, searching for the object of his trip.

"Do you have reservations?" Shawna was asking.

He looked at her gloomily. "No, I'm afraid we don't. Will you be able to fit us in?"

She looked doubtful, studying the seating chart. "I don't know. We're awfully crowded tonight. I'm afraid it will be at least an hour wait if you—"

"An hour!" Pica screeched. "Oh, I'm starving, Jimmy. I can't wait an hour!" James was trying to quiet her, when a voice cut in like the sound of a bell.

"Let me handle this, Shawna."

James turned and for a moment, he couldn't believe his eyes. It was Kyra all right, but it was a different Kyra from the one he'd seen at work. That one was a lovely woman, but a businesslike figure of dignity and modesty. This one, in her tight dress and her four-inch heels, had a body made of dangerous curves with a cleavage that seemed to beg for a visual caress. The face was flushed, the lips pouty, the dark eyes smoldering, and the hair... His mouth went dry at the sight of her.

"Hello, Mr. Redman," she was saying calmly, her eyes sliding sideways to take a quick look at Pica. "I think I can find a table for you. Come this way."

She started off into a side dining area and he followed, taking in the sway of her rounded bottom as though he'd never seen a woman walk before. When she stopped at a table tucked into a side spot, he was so involved in watching her move, he almost ran her down and had to mutter an apology as she pointed out the chair he could pull out for his date. Pica was still talking. In fact, she was talking to Kyra, complimenting her on the flower behind her ear, asking her some question about the birdcalls in the background, but James wasn't listening. He was still trying to recover from his first sight of Kyra. And he was beginning to realize that might take some doing.

He sat and she put a menu in his hands, but he couldn't take his gaze off her.

She gave him a cool look that told him she wasn't exactly thrilled he'd come into her other place of work. "Enjoy your dinner," she said, and then she was walking away, and he got another view of that fabulous posterior. It was a good thing he was sitting, because there was a definite weakness in his knees. Pica was babbling on about her trip to Hawaii six months before. He took a long drink of the cold water the waiter had set down before him and came to the realization that he hadn't told Kyra he wanted to talk to her again. He hadn't, in fact, gotten one intelligent word out from the moment he'd laid eyes on her. Good heavens. He'd been acting like a complete idiot.

"What are you going to have?" Pica was asking, completely oblivious to his muddled state. "I think I'll try the mahimahi in macadamia nut crust with pineapple butter on the side. What do you think?"

He thought there was too much noise in this restaurant, making it impossible to think. The other diners were laughing and talking all around them and the damn birds were caterwauling along with the tropical chanting and bongo drums. And he thought he caught the sound of a polka somewhere off in the distance. A polka? That didn't fit. Must be his imagination.

"I want a steak," he growled. "Rare."

"Then why did we come to a Polynesian place?" Pica asked innocently.

He didn't bother to answer, but she didn't notice. She'd already started a new conversation about rain forest insects and slimy things that one might find in the food when traveling in tropical countries. He knew she would be perfectly happy to talk for another half hour without any input from him, so he ignored her and concentrated on what he was going to say to Kyra when he finally got her alone. The prospect had his palms sweating.

The waiter took their order and brought the appetizer special Kyra had sent them. Pica oohed and aahed over it but never bothered to ask where it had come from or why Kyra would send it. James stared at the plate of sizzling bits of tempura and glanced at his watch.

"Uh, excuse me, Pica," he said, breaking into her expository piece on the virtues of deep-frying, "I've got to go make a phone call."

"Don't you have your cellular phone with you?"

"No. I left it in the car." He rose and put down his napkin.

She looked lost for a few seconds. Whom was she going to talk to? Just in time, a woman at the next table leaned over and asked if she could borrow the candle on theirs to relight her candle, and Pica was off and running once again, completely happy. James left her without a qualm.

Kyra was doing deep-breathing exercises. She had to calm down. It was frantic around the restaurant at this time of night, but that was no excuse for feeling as though she were on some kind of mind-altering drug. She knew the cause. James Redman was in the building.

That fact alone wouldn't have thrown her off this way, she told herself sternly, if only she'd been warned and had had time to prepare. But to walk into her familiar area of work and find him standing there, looking incredibly handsome in a crisp black suit more formal than the one he usually wore to Tri-TerraCorp, with that head-turningly beautiful woman

in the scanty, abdomen-revealing excuse for a dress
on his arm, had been a little too much to laugh off.

She was still angry with him. But she had no doubt
he'd come tonight because she'd mentioned that she
worked here. So he couldn't have dismissed her from
his mind quite so thoroughly as he'd pretended that
afternoon. Had he come to look over her workplace
to see if this was a job she would give up his offer
for? Or had he come to mock her, since that seemed
to be one of his hobbies?

She said good-night to Gayle and her husband as
they were leaving, then found one of the waiters gesturing to her.

"What is it, Bobby?" she asked, hurrying over.

"The party in the Aloha Room," Bobby huffed at
her. "Haven't you noticed the noise they're making?
Customers are complaining."

Lifting her head, she heard what he was talking
about and wondered how she could have missed it
before. The accordion players were getting quite en-
thusiastic. The polka tunes were interfering with the
Polynesian mood music. It was obvious something
had to be done at once.

"I'll take care of it," she assured the young man,
and started toward the banquet rooms. As she approached the music got louder and louder, and en-
ergetic shouts began to punctuate the verses.

"All in a night's work," she muttered to herself
grimly as she threw open the door to the room and
was almost bowled over by the wave of joyous sound
that hit her—as well as the riotous colors of the cos-
tumes the accordion buffs and their dates were wearing. The party was in full swing, with a line of danc-
ers sashaying around the room. The poor waiters

were trying to dodge revelers as they began to put food on the table. The scene was in desperate need of a manager. But there was no manager in sight, so a hostess would have to do.

"That's me," she told herself with a sigh. Going to the front of the room, she grabbed the microphone away from the main singer.

"Hey, everybody," she ordered in her best military manner. "Listen up!"

Ten minutes later, she was back at the front desk, holding back exhaustion. Finding James standing there, restlessly waiting for her didn't help.

"I've got to talk to you," he said, his turquoise eyes shining in the dim light.

"I'm working," she told him, brushing right past him and smiling at a couple who were waiting at the desk. "Two? Your name, please?"

He waited while she dealt with the customers. "I'm serious," he said as soon as she was free again. "I have something I need to explain to you."

"I'm a little busy. Can't it wait until tomorrow?"

"No." He glanced around to make sure no one overheard them. "I've had an idea. A second job that would be less stressful and pay better than this, as well as leaving you free to take the position I've offered you at TriTerraCorp."

"You've found me another job?" She gazed at him, amazed. Did he really think he could just walk in and take over her life? She shook her head. "Mr. Redman, go eat your dinner." She began to turn away but he grabbed her arm to keep her close.

"I think you'll be interested in this," he told her. "I need a chance to present it properly."

"Okay," she said, looking him squarely in the eye. "Shoot."

He hesitated. "Not here. You'll be interrupted. What time do you get off?"

She raised an eyebrow. "You have a date with you," she reminded him.

He frowned. "She's not really a date. Don't worry. I'll get rid of her."

Suspicions confirmed. He looked at women as expendable toys. She resisted the impulse to kick him in the shin.

He must have sensed her reaction to his statement because he made a quick amendment. "She's just an old friend from Dallas. I told her I had things to do after dinner. I'll take her to her hotel and then I'll be back."

"I don't get off until eleven."

"I'll be here."

"No, Mr. Redman. Really, I can't. I have a woman staying with my grandmother and I have to get home right away, as soon as I get off, to let her go home."

His brows drew together and his mouth tightened. "Get off early, then." He turned on his heel to return to his table. "I'll be back at ten," he threw over his shoulder as he left.

She shook her head. "No, I can't...."

But he was already gone. She watched his wide shoulders disappear into the next room and swallowed hard. She knew she could get off at ten if she really wanted to. Things would have died way down by then, and Shawna would cover for her. But did she want to do that? She bit her lip, wondering.

But not for long. Bobby, the waiter, was back. "The accordion guys are going wild again," he told her, his flat, wide face crinkled with worry. "When I tried to quiet them down, they all started throwing cookies at me." He gave her a look that told her he'd been mortally offended and shook his head like a dog after a swim. Cookie crumbs flew in all directions.

Kyra sighed. "All right. I'll take care of them." She squared her shoulders and started for the banquet room. Why was it so easy for her to get tough with unruly customers, but so hard to talk back to James Redman?

Chapter Four

Kyra sat in the Porsche and felt as though she wanted to grab hold of the seat as James took tight corners. He hadn't said a word since they'd left the restaurant. It felt very odd to be riding in a fancy sports car with a TriTerraCorp executive. Wasn't this the sort of thing mothers warned their daughters about?

She was trying to relax, but he was making it difficult. It had been a pretty hectic evening at the restaurant. Between dealing with James and taming the accordion players, she was worn to a frazzle. She'd had some success with the musicians, but she'd had to promise to do one polka turn of the room with the leader, and when they'd finished, he'd fallen on one knee and proposed on the spot. She had to smile now, thinking about it. Her first proposal, made by a man in a puffy yellow shirt and purple bell-bottoms. Maybe she should have taken him up on it. Would that be like running away to join the circus?

James took another sharp corner and they were on Ocean Boulevard. The night was clear and a full moon was spilling silver across the inky sea. He pulled into the parking lot at the pier and turned off the engine, vaulting out of the car and coming to her side.

"Let's take a walk," he said, holding her door open and offering her a hand.

She rose from the passenger's seat and looked around. She'd never been to the pier so late at night but what she saw reassured her. There was plenty of activity. Little clusters of family groups carrying pails and fishing rods were scattered here and there, and a parade of couples, mostly college age, were sauntering the length of the old wooden structure. She pulled her coat around her shoulders, guarding against the cool night breeze, and gave James a quick smile.

"Fine," she told him.

They walked out on the boardwalk for ten minutes before they found a place where they could lean against the railing and look down at where the water lapped relentlessly against the wood pilings, crashing across the beds of black mussels bristling like ancient crusts around the thick wooden posts.

James put both hands on the heavy railing and leaned out, staring down into the water. "Do you like the sea?" he asked her.

She looked at him, bemused by his question. "I've lived in a beach town all my life," she said. "It's like air, like sunshine. It's part of me."

He nodded, and she wasn't sure if it was because he agreed with her, or because he was just acknowledging her view of things. "I grew up not far from here," he said softly. "In Santa Barbara."

"I didn't know that." She looked at him, thinking how handsome he looked with the breeze tossing his thick dark hair. "Then getting transferred here was like coming home."

"In a way. I haven't really lived here since I went away to college."

"Oh."

He turned his head and looked at her. "So you live with your grandmother?"

"Yes." She nodded. "She's not very well. My parents were killed in a plane accident about six years ago and I've lived with my grandparents ever since." She looked down at the restless water. "My grandfather died a little over two years ago. So my grandmother and I just have each other."

He frowned. "You don't have any other family?"

"No one close. Why?"

He suddenly looked totally innocent. "No reason. I was just wondering."

She didn't buy the innocent routine, but she wasn't going to call him a liar. So far, he had completely confused her as to why they were there at all. And she had to admit, she was very wary. He'd said he wanted to tell her about a job. Well, why didn't he get to it? She was beginning to wonder if he really had something else in mind, and it made her very nervous. She didn't want to have an awkward scene. Conversation, she supposed. That was the key.

"How about you?" she asked him. "Do you have any family left in Santa Barbara?"

He took a deep breath and looked restive, as though he wanted to walk again, but instead, he turned his back to the railing and leaned against it, folding his arms across his chest. "Well, that was one of the things I wanted to tell you about," he said mysteriously. "You see, I lost my parents too, only it happened when I was very young. My father's sister, Josephine Redman, took me and raised me in Santa Barbara. Aunt Jo, I call her." He stared at her, as though he were trying to tell her something on another level, something deeper than his words.

She nodded helpfully.

"I really care about her," he said earnestly, as though she'd scoffed at the notion.

"Of course," she replied. She frowned slightly. She wished she knew what he was trying to say, but she didn't have a clue.

He looked unhappy with her answer and straightened, reaching out to grab her hand. "Come on," he said. "Let's get a cup of coffee."

His hand was warm and felt natural holding hers as they walked through the cool ocean breeze. He led her to a diner at the end of the pier. The place was almost empty. They chose a booth that would have looked out over the water if it had been day, and still gave a glimpse of moon-tipped waves now and then. They slid into seats across from each other. The waiter slapped two cups of coffee down in front of them.

"Okay, let me start this over again," James said once they'd settled. "My father was a career navy man. He was on his second tour of duty in Vietnam when my mother went to Hawaii to meet him during his R and R, leaving me with my Aunt Jo. They hired a boat and went out into the ocean and never came back. Their bodies were never found, but they were presumed dead. I was four.''

Kyra shuddered. This was similar to what had happened to her, only worse. At least she'd been old enough to deal with it. ''Oh, how horrible.''

He shrugged away her sympathy. ''I don't really remember it. But my Aunt Jo was all I had left. She had never married. She never wanted children. She was an archaeologist, and becoming quite famous in her field at the time. She consulted all over the world and the last thing she needed was a four-year-old kid to take care of.'' His face took on a sentimental softness all of a sudden as he thought of his aunt and what she'd done for him. ''She could have given me up for adoption. Or put me in a boarding school. Or found some obscure relative she could have paid to take me. But she didn't.'' He took a deep breath and gazed deep into Kyra's eyes. ''She put her career on hold for twelve years so that she could stay home and raise me. She did it because she loved her brother, and loved me by extension, and was bound and determined to do what was best for me.''

It was a touching story and she could see that it stirred something deep in him to tell it. But for the life of her, she couldn't understand why he felt so compelled to tell her about it. She murmured sympathetic things, but she was waiting for the other shoe to drop. She was sure there would be one.

He read her mind. ''Okay, you're wondering why I'm telling you this. I do have a reason.'' But he hesitated, and his gaze shifted and he swore softly under his breath so that she couldn't hear it. What had seemed so logical when he'd thought of it now seemed quirky and contrived. He was on the verge of losing his nerve. "Do you want something to eat?" he asked her, vamping for time. "How about a piece of pie?"

She shook her head, frowning. "I'm not hungry. And I do have to get home soon. So..."

"Okay, okay." He tried to smile at her, but that felt even phonier so he gazed earnestly into her eyes instead. "Here's the deal. I told you I had an idea about a better second job for you."

She nodded, her eyes bright but wary. When he'd first brought it up, she'd been outraged that he had the audacity to try to plan her life for her. But she'd had second thoughts. After all, he seemed to be doing it because he really did want her to take the job administering his special project. That was flattering, she supposed. And it was obvious he was going through a lot to present his idea to her. She had to give him credit for that. Still, why did all this have to be such a mystery? "Does this have anything to do with the company?"

"Uh...only indirectly." He cleared his throat and tapped his fingertips on the Formica top of the table between them. "I'll get to those details in a moment." He looked up at her expectantly. "First, I want you to understand that this is a temporary position, which is projected to last exactly six months. But it will pay very well. The salary will be three times what you make at TriTerraCorp."

"Three times?" Her eyes widened. She wasn't making much, but three times of not much ended up being a pretty nice amount. Enough, in fact, to get her out of debt very quickly. Enough to find her grandmother a proper nursing home.... Her heart thumped and she had to take a deep breath.

"Three times," he repeated, looking glad to have found something that perked up her ears. "And you'll still be working at TriTerraCorp. And with your promotion there..."

"Wait a minute." She shook her head. When things sounded too good to be true, they almost always were. "I'm not sure I understand. Just what would this job entail? What would I be doing every day?"

He blinked at her, but didn't really answer. "I want to stress that this will be a major commitment," he said instead. "A full-time job. But because of the nature of it, as you'll understand in a moment, it will dovetail perfectly with your regular job, so..."

Curiouser and curiouser. She felt about ready to scream. Why couldn't he just come right out and tell her what it was? She leaned forward to interrupt him. "You say full time. What exactly do you mean by full time?"

"I mean completely full time. Twenty-four hours a day."

Her fingers tightened on the edge of the table. She tried to think what sort of job would require her for twenty-four hours. "That's impossible," she said breathlessly.

"That's the job."

She frowned, feeling adrift in choppy water, and her voice rose as she demanded, "What exactly *is* the job?"

There it was again—a funny shift in his gaze. Just as she suspected, something fishy was going on. She tensed and waited to hear what it was.

His smile looked less confident than usual. "It's going to sound a little strange..." he began, then hesitated, looking almost embarrassed. "Okay, here it is. You'll be working for me. I need...that is...oh, what the hell. It's like this." He looked at her fiercely. "I need a wife right away."

Her jaw dropped.

"I know it's unusual," he said quickly. "But you see, as I explained, I adore my aunt. I owe her everything. I would do anything for her. Except...except what she wants me to do. Right now, my aunt is pressuring me to marry someone I can't stand, but she's mainly doing it because she just wants me married and if I marry someone else, she'll have to give up on that other person."

She took the deepest breath yet and let it out again, shaking her head, feeling shell-shocked. Suddenly she had the urge to laugh. "I don't believe this."

"And, like I said," he went on, ignoring her comment, "I don't want to get married at all. Not ever. It's not in my blueprint for my life. Never has been. So I hit upon this plan. I'm going to hire a woman to marry me for one year. We'll live together, but no one will know we are actually married in name only. At the end of the year, we'll part company, get a no-fault divorce, annulment, whatever, and go on our merry ways."

She didn't know whether to laugh or cry. Was this an insult? Or a compliment? The man was crazy. Boss or no boss, someone needed to set him straight. She shook her head, looking at him in wonder. Could he really be serious? Then she remembered what he'd done to her that afternoon—how he'd drawn her in only to leave her high and dry. She'd better be careful, she told herself. For all she knew, he might be doing it again. She wasn't going to fall for it a second time.

She set her lips, then said tartly, "Mr. Redman, I know you're new in town, but you don't need to do this. You're a…a very attractive man. Surely you can get a date without going to these lengths."

He shook his head, slightly annoyed that she wasn't getting it. "It's not a date that I'm looking for."

"You could have fooled me." She gathered her purse and pulled her coat around her, ready to make a run for it. "But don't worry. Almost any of the young, single women at TriTerraCorp would be happy to go out with you." She rose. "I just don't happen to be one of them."

He stared at her, his face imperious and definitely annoyed. "You don't understand. I don't want to go out with anyone. I'm looking for a business partner, not a sex partner."

The man was a maniac. She glanced at her watch. It was almost eleven. She had to get home.

"If you've got some time tomorrow," he was saying, "I'd like to take you over and show you the apartment where we would be living."

Oh sure. Right. And maybe his etchings, too. Her chin rose and she glared at him. "That's just the problem, Mr. Redman. I don't have the time." She turned to leave, but he was out of his seat and standing in her way before she'd taken two steps.

"You have a prior engagement?" he asked coolly.

"I have a life. I'm too busy. I have too many responsibilities of my own to have any time left over to play house with you." She took another step toward the door and he grabbed her arm, stopping her cold.

"Were you listening to what I've been saying?" he demanded, anger brewing in his turquoise gaze.

"Yes. I've listened to every word. I've got to hand it to you. You've come up with the most annoyingly inventive way of getting a cheap date I've ever heard of."

His hand tightened on her arm and his gaze hardened. "That is not what I'm doing here."

"Isn't it?"

"No."

His hand on her arm was like a brand, hot and unbelievably disturbing. And the look in his eyes was evidence that he was telling the truth when he insisted on his seriousness. But she couldn't trust him. Not yet. Bad things seemed to happen whenever she trusted a man.

"You expect me to believe that you want me to marry you for one year to keep your aunt off your back? I'm sorry Mr. Redman. This just doesn't fly."

He gazed at her speculatively. "Maybe if you met my Aunt Jo—"

She put up a hand as if to stop any more nonsense. "I don't want to meet any of your relatives."

"I've only got the one."

She threw him an exasperated glance. "Just one? Is that why you're trolling for more?"

To her surprise, he smiled. "You've got a sense of humor," he noted dryly. "That's a bonus."

His smile was deadly. It scared her much more than his frown ever could. "Mr. Redman," she began, pulling away from his touch.

"Miss Symington," he said, dropping his hand. "Please hear me out."

Something in his voice stopped her. He really seemed to mean it. She hesitated, not sure if she should make her way quickly out the door and call for a cab or wait for a fuller explanation.

"Hold on a minute," he said, taking money out of his pocket and tossing it down on the table. "Let's go. Don't worry. I'll get you back in time."

They walked back along the pier, but this time he didn't try to hold her hand. He was wondering if he'd done the right thing. When it had come to him that afternoon, it had seemed the perfect solution and he didn't know why he hadn't thought of it before. He needed a wife but he didn't really want to get married. At the same time, there were women out there who needed jobs. Simple as that. Purely business. The free market system in action. Everyone won.

Are you crazy? a little voice inside his head had said that afternoon when he'd been plotting this, a voice that stood for all his friends, all his co-workers, everyone who knew him and had any sense at all. *You can't do that!*

"Oh yeah?" he'd said aloud to them all. "Just watch me."

"Did you call, Mr. Redman?" Ginny, the mail-room clerk had asked, looking into his office with a worried frown.

"No, Ginny," he'd said, holding back the growl he felt like using. It was no use to show disapproval. Even the slightest hint of criticism made the poor thing tear up. And if there was anything he hated, it was a female who used tears to get softer treatment. He'd had recent and painful experience with a woman who cried all the time. He had shirts that were still wet.

He stole a glance at Kyra, judging her. No, this one wasn't a crier. This one had a lot of qualities he really liked—at least at first glance. Time would tell, he supposed, if she was as pushy and greedy as most of the women he'd dated in his life.

"You've got to give this some thought," he told her solemnly. "I need a wife for exactly the reasons I've stated. I have no ulterior motives. I do not plan to take advantage of a husband's prerogatives. I just need someone to help me for one year."

He glanced sideways at her, then reached out and put a hand at the back of her neck, guiding her past a rowdy group of teenagers who were good-naturedly pushing one another toward the railing, acting like a pack of big puppies. When they'd passed the boys, he dropped his hand, and she felt suddenly cool, missing his warm touch on her neck.

"In return," he went on, "you'll receive a lavish salary and a lot of free time. I will require you to accompany me to various company and social functions. There may even be a time or two when I would need you to act as hostess for a dinner or a party. And that is it. We will both sign a contract to that effect. If you like, bring your own lawyer to look it over. I assure you, it will be most generous."

For one long, shimmering moment, she thought maybe she believed him, and she actually considered it. He seemed so sincere, so open, and she felt the pull of his charisma as she'd never felt it before. The life he outlined sounded, in many ways, ideal. To think of living in what she was sure was a wonderful, luxurious apartment, having everything available that a woman could want. And the money! To have enough to pay the bills!

Mentally, she shook herself. If she didn't watch out, she would get carried away here. Bottom line— the whole idea was crazy—a Cinderella dream. But life wasn't like fairy tales. And she had to get home.

Once they were in the car again, he turned to her before starting the engine. He knew she was confused and rather disturbed by his idea. His impulse was to tell her to trust him, but when you came right down to it, why should she?

"I know this seems a preposterous idea to you at the moment," he said quietly. "All I ask is that you think it over. Once you get more used to it, you might have a different reaction."

She looked at his handsome face, shadowed strangely by the streetlight. "Why me?" she asked him. "What made you think..." Her voice trailed off and she shrugged as words failed her.

"I like you," he said. It was the truth.

But it didn't really answer her question. "Why not...why not someone you've dated, like that woman who was with you at the restaurant?"

"Pica?" He groaned, rolling his head back against the headrest. "Pica drives me nuts. She never shuts up." He raised his head and looked at her with casual approval. "You, on the other hand, have a nice calm quietness about you. On the ride over here from the restaurant, you didn't say a word." He smiled at her. "I like that in a woman."

She sighed her exasperation with his answer. "That's hardly a reason to marry someone."

"It's much more important than you think. You're a rare find. Most women I've met seem to feel they have to provide a running narrative of their life and of all the lives around them, everywhere they go.''

She couldn't hold back a smile. ''That's called being communicative.''

''I call it being a pain in the neck.''

She bit her lip. ''Maybe I'm just too scared of you to say anything,'' she proposed softly.

''Scared?'' He ground out the word, raising his voice. ''Why on earth would you be scared?''

She met his gaze, her eyes bubbling with amusement, and he got the joke right away. ''Sorry,'' he muttered. ''I didn't mean to yell at you.'' He looked her over, then added, ''But don't try to get away with that 'scared' stuff. You've stood up to me from the first. You're no shrinking violet.''

No, she wasn't. But she was no brave pioneer, either. And she wasn't about to stick her neck out. He was going to have to convince her, and she wasn't at all sure that was possible.

He shifted back in his seat and turned the key in the ignition, starting the engine. Looking for traffic, he turned out onto Ocean Boulevard and began the return trip to the restaurant where her car was parked.

''Look,'' he went on. ''I'd been agonizing over what to do about this problem for the past few days, and I'd started thinking about hiring someone to be my wife for a year. But it seemed just as nutty to me at first as it does to you now.''

She glanced over at him, then looked again, caught by the strength of his profile. She realized she'd never known a man who looked better. It was really sort of dismaying how nice it was to look at a handsome man. After all, his character should be the most important thing—and was. But good looks sure did help.

"After you left my office this afternoon," he continued, "the idea came to me out of the blue." He hit the steering wheel with the flat of his hand as though showing her just how it was. "And it seemed crazy. But the more I thought about it, the more I realized how brilliant it was. You see, if I make it completely a business transaction, if I hired someone I don't really know, but whom I got along with pretty well, it might actually work."

He glanced over to see if she was listening—if she understood what a revelation this was to him. "There would be no old baggage to get in the way. No secret expectations. No unfulfilled promises. Everything would be under contract and aboveboard. Everything spelled out clearly." He shrugged, turning a corner and merging their vehicle into traffic. "It couldn't be simpler."

Simple? The man called this a simple plan? What was simple about marrying someone? Did he really think he could control human emotions by putting everything in a contract?

Suddenly, Kyra began to laugh. He glanced over at her, ready to be offended.

"Sorry," she told him, stifling the amusement that filled her. "I just realized something. After a lifetime of drought, I've had two proposals in one night." She told him about what had happened with the accordion player.

He chuckled. "Well, it's up to you. It's either the corporate world, or life in a gypsy caravan. Your choice."

He pulled up next to her car and she turned to

look at him. "I'm afraid I'm going to have to say neither of the above," she told him, bracing herself for an argument and reaching for the handle on the door so that she could escape.

"Not yet." He dismissed her words with a jerk of his head. "You can't make a decision yet. You need time to think about it." He pressed a card into her hand. "My home number. Give me a call any time you want to talk it over."

She took the card and slid out of the car, but she turned just before closing the door. "Mr. Redman, there is no use in you waiting for me to call. I can't do this. I have too many responsibilities. I'm afraid you are going to have to find someone else."

His eyes seemed to glow in the late-night shadows. "I don't want someone else," he said softly. "I want *you.*"

She stared at him for a moment, her heart thumping loudly in her chest. For just a moment, she'd thought he actually meant...but he couldn't have. This was just a business deal. That's what he'd said all along.

"Meet me tomorrow for breakfast at the Waffle House on Olvera Street," he told her. "Seven o'clock. We'll talk more then."

"But, Mr. Redman..."

"And start calling me James, at least when we're not at work," he told her. "See you tomorrow at the Waffle House." Reaching out, he pulled the door closed, and then he drove the car back along the curb where he could watch until she was safely in her car and on her way.

She sighed, giving in to exasperation and fatigue.

A night of thinking this over wasn't going to make any difference. It couldn't change her situation at home. But at least, after some rest, she might be able to put up a better fight. She certainly hoped so.

Chapter Five

She drove home, making the moves automatically, her mind on what had happened, her emotions alternating wildly between fury and wonder. How did people even think of things like this? How could he have imagined she might go along? How could he be so arrogant? It was beyond belief, like nothing she'd ever come across before. You couldn't do that. You couldn't just marry as a business transaction.

Could you?

But enough of that nonsense. She was late. She hated the way she always seemed to be late for everything these days. She hated most of all to make Nurse O'Brien wait this late at night. The woman was so good and did a wonderful job taking care of her grandmother. If they lost Nurse O'Brien, she didn't know what she'd do.

She pulled into the driveway and rushed into the little house, calling out a greeting as she dumped her coat on a chair and headed for the back bedroom

where her grandmother now spent almost all of her
time.

The dear elderly lady lay back against the white
pillows, her face creased in a smile as she reached
out to receive her granddaughter's embrace.

"You darling girl, you work so hard," she sighed
as Kyra drew back. "I wish you would find some
nice young man to take care of you. You certainly
deserve a little help these days."

"Young men aren't like they used to be, Grandmother. Nowadays they expect the women to take
care of them." She smiled at the older woman. "And
all I want to do is take care of you." She looked
around. "Where is Nurse O'Brien?"

"She had to leave."

Kyra whirled and stared down at her. "What? She
left you all alone?"

"Now, Kyra, I made her go. She had a family
emergency. And I can take care of myself for a few
hours, for heaven's sake." As if to give lie to her
words, her energy seemed to run out at that very
moment, and she closed her eyes, gathering her
strength.

Kyra's own eyes filled with tears. It was very hard
seeing her this way and remembering the happy, vi-
brant woman she'd been up until about a year earlier.
She would give anything to bring back her grandmother's health for her.

The doctor said she really belonged in a well-
maintained nursing home, with medical attention
available at all hours, physical therapists and activi-
ties and programs for keeping the infirm interested
and active. Her grandmother's friend Hilda was in
just such a place. Hilda's phone calls made them all

jealous as she went on and on about what a wonderful home her son Bertie had found for her. But Bertie was a senior partner in his law firm. He could afford the best. Kyra couldn't even afford Nurse O'Brien, when she came right down to it.

Her thoughts strayed to James and his proposal. With the kind of money he was talking about, maybe she could... No, she wasn't going to think that way. What James had proposed was impossible. A pipe dream. She might as well pin her hopes on winning the lottery.

"At any rate, I'm going to have to get used to being alone more often," her grandmother said weakly, opening her eyes again. "Once Nurse O'Brien leaves..."

"Leaves? What are you talking about?"

"Weren't you listening? She told you all about it when you came home to change for the restaurant."

Kyra put her hands to her face. "I...I was so rushed. I didn't really hear what she was saying."

The woman looked lovingly at her granddaughter.

"Then I'll tell you. She's had a letter from her sister in Alabama. The sister is having foot surgery in a couple of weeks and is going to need Nurse O'Brien to come help with her children while she's laid up. Nurse O'Brien will be gone at least three months. Don't look so stricken, Kyra. It can't be helped. We can hire a local teenager to look in on me after school."

Kyra wanted to say, "Not on your life!" But she couldn't, because it just might come down to that. Panic fluttered in her chest. She couldn't bear to think of her grandmother being left alone, and she couldn't afford to put her in a decent home. What was she going to do?

She stayed at her grandmother's bedside for a few more minutes, forcing herself to put aside her despair so that it couldn't be detected in her voice. She talked to the older woman quietly until she began to fall asleep. Just as she was tucking the covers in around her, she heard her grandmother say softly, "If only you would get married. Then I would have peace...."

She bit her lip, holding back tears. Moving slowly, as though her body ached, she turned off the light and went to her own room, stripping off her dress as soon as she entered, releasing herself from the trappings of her evening. Was it just her imagination, or was everything in the universe conspiring to get her married? She couldn't wait to get into bed and fall asleep and leave all this confusion behind for a few hours. And tomorrow, she had a date for breakfast.

James sat waiting in the most private booth at the Waffle House, tucked back in a corner out of the way of the bustling breakfast crowd. He'd been up early taking Pica to the airport. She'd been a little pouty when he'd tried to explain he wanted her to go back to Dallas because he just didn't have time to pay enough attention to her to make her happy. She wasn't dumb. She knew something was up. But it was just as well.

He shot back his cuff and studied his watch, then glanced at his half-empty coffee cup and frowned. Kyra was late. Did that mean she wasn't going to show up?

For the first time, he let himself entertain the pos-

RAYE MORGAN   73

sibility that she might turn down his marriage
scheme. What was he going to do if that were the
case? Did he have a second choice in marriage-
business partners?

Not a chance. He knew a lot of women, even some
in the area, though he'd only been in town for a few
weeks. He still had contact with plenty of his past
dates and friends in Dallas, not to mention those he'd
known in college. And there wasn't one he'd ever
consider spending the next year attached to.

He groaned, lolling back in his seat and playing
with the spoon. He really hated the idea of getting
married. He'd had a few lovers in his time, women
who had professed themselves crazy about him, but
he'd never felt truly and deeply loved. All his life
women had been attracted to him. He knew he was
good looking. He'd had enough evidence of it.
Women were drawn to him at first because of his
handsome face, but once they got close and found
out about his position and wealth, they were usually
hooked. He couldn't count the women who had
thrown themselves at him, hoping to land him like a
big shiny fish. But it was all surface. They didn't
ever dig deep.

And that was part of the reason he'd never felt any
woman had loved him. Not really. Not for what he
was rather than what he could give her or make her
feel like. He'd had lovers but no real love. He hadn't
felt really happy or satisfied with any of his relation-
ships.

But when he came right down to it, he'd never
loved someone with any overarching passion. He'd
never felt he couldn't live without any of the women
he'd romanced. He wasn't sure there was really such

a thing as that sort of love. He knew about the kind
he had for his Aunt Jo, and the kind she had for him.
They had a tie of affection and lifelong commitment
that he cherished. But he didn't have to see her every
morning before he'd brushed his teeth. He didn't
have to get her permission before he decided to run
off to New Orleans for the weekend. He didn't have
to promise never to look at another aunt. And if he
got tired of her, he could always go off and not see
her for months at a time. You couldn't do that with
a wife.

But all this was coming dangerously close to self-
pity and he hated whining. What the hell. Maybe the
women he dated didn't dig deep because there was
nothing deeper. Maybe he was too superficial to in-
spire the sort of depth he seemed to crave. And
maybe all he was doing was blowing hot air.

But all that was irrelevant now. He'd offered Kyra
the job and he still had very little doubt that she
would take it. He'd studied her résumé and thought
he knew a lot about her background. If he knew
women, she would jump at the chance to live the sort
of life he was offering her. He just hoped she turned
out to be what he needed—and mostly that she would
leave him alone.

Funny. He didn't know why, but Kyra was the
only woman he'd met since he'd become an adult
who seemed like he might be able to take over a
long haul. She just had the quiet sort of self-
possession you didn't often find. Plus she was pretty
as a picture, with curves to match and with great hair.
But that wasn't the point, he told himself hurriedly.
Because this wasn't going to be a sexual relationship.
No, that would only complicate things and he knew

it. He and Kyra were going to have to live together like brother and sister. And pretend to be husband and wife.

"Hi," she said, hurrying up. "Sorry I'm late."

He favored her with a long, slow smile as he looked her over. She was wearing a sweater and skirt combination that hugged her breasts in a way that made him squirm in his seat. Her hair was free and soft around her face, and her cheeks were flushed. Watching her as she took her seat opposite his, he had a strong, urgent impulse to kiss her to get a taste of what she might be like on a hot summer night....

But he couldn't do that, so he consoled himself with a long, lingering look at her full, provocative lips. A man could dream, couldn't he?

"Hello." She waved a hand in front of his face. "Are you awake?"

"Oh yes," he said, his voice almost a purr.

She looked worried, as though she could sense there was something going on she didn't quite get, yet knew she wouldn't like if she knew about it. But she took a sip of the orange juice already sitting at her place and put the napkin in her lap.

"You wanted to discuss your crazy idea," she reminded him. "We'll have to discuss fast. I'm due in at work—"

"At whatever time I decide you should be there," he finished for her. "I'm the boss. Remember?"

That put her back up. She glared at him. "Yes, sir," she said, letting a hint of sarcasm color her tone. "And I suppose you'd bring that up all the time if I did agree to marry you."

He saw where this was going and cursed himself for having started them down this track. "No, no, not at all," he reassured her. "I'm sorry I said that. I was just being flip." Reaching out, he took her hand in his and gazed earnestly into her eyes. "Believe me, we'll be equals in the marriage. I'll never pull rank. We can put it in the contract."

She had to smile at a man having so much faith in a simple piece of paper with words on it. "Well, never mind that," she told him breezily, pulling her hand from his and breaking off a corner of his piece of toast before popping it into her mouth. "Because we're not going to be married. So the point is a moot one."

He frowned. "What do you need to convince you?" he asked.

She shook her head, but the waitress appeared before she could answer him. She ordered a bagel and cream cheese, then turned back to James. "The whole idea is ridiculous. It will never work. We would never convince anyone."

"Oh yeah?"

"Yeah."

"What makes you so sure?"

"Common sense. That is the one thing I have a lot of."

"How about some imagination, instead?"

"I've got plenty of that, too, and I can imagine a lot of things that could go wrong."

He merely looked bored. "Name your objections. I'll deal with them one by one."

She took a deep breath. "First off, if I did marry you, I wouldn't be able to take the job administering your project. It would be seen as nepotism, granting favors. People would whisper about me sleeping my way up the ladder, and about you being unprofessional.''

"I've thought of that," he admitted. "But there's a way around it."

"What's that?"

"I didn't come here to handle Special Projects. I was supposed to take over Contract Negotiations from Fred Weems when I transferred from Dallas. My expertise is actually in closing deals. I got here and found out Fred had two months to go before his retirement, and he didn't want to hand over the reins just yet. I took over Special Projects as an interim appointment. As usual, it was a screwup at the board level.'' He shook his head. "They never know what's going on. Within the month I'm handing Projects over to Kurt Barbour and taking over Negotiations, where I belong.'' He shrugged. "So you see, I won't be your direct supervisor. No one will be able to say anything.''

She marvelled at the man. Everything seemed so easy to him. All he did was snap his fingers and things fell into place the way he wanted them. The waitress arrived with her bagel and she took a bite. She felt as though she needed some fortification.

"Okay," he said. "Next?"

She blinked. She'd thought she had a winner there, but if he needed something else, that shouldn't be so hard to find. "I have my grandmother to think of. She has diabetes. She needs constant care.''

"Bring her along. My apartment has five bedrooms. We'll hire around-the-clock medical care.'' His smug smile was infuriating. "Next?"

Her mind was blank all of a sudden. There had to be a great argument. Logic suggested as much. But she couldn't find it at the moment. Instead, she went with another angle.

"I'll tell you one thing. I'm still having a hard time believing the underlying premise of your proposal. I understand that you love your aunt and that she wants you to marry very badly. But who is this woman she wants you to marry? Why do you have this intense reaction against her?"

The good-natured look vanished from his face and his eyes turned steely. "Jalopy Clark," he said, his voice dripping venom. "Her mother and my aunt were best friends, and they lived with us on and off from the time I was eight until sometime after my thirteenth birthday, when they went to live in Australia. I was saddled with that little brat all my growing-up years. I couldn't stand her...." Pure loathing choked him.

"She was just your age?"

"Two years younger." His eyes took on a faraway look as he remembered. "A nasty little freckle-faced brat. She had a nose like Porky Pig. She followed me everywhere. She ruined my childhood."

Kyra hid a grin and tried to maintain a solemn tone. "What on earth did she do to make you so furious with her?"

He looked grouchy. "The details are unimportant."

No, the details were everything! She had to know. "Did she tease you? Hide your baseball cards? Tell your secrets to your friends? Tell on you to your aunt?"

"All of the above. In spades. Not only did she tag along everywhere I went and make me miserable, she would taunt bigger boys until they would come after her and then I would have to go out and defend her. She caused me so many bloody noses—''

"Like any little sister."

His turquoise eyes glittered dangerously. "No sister of mine would ever have been that vicious. The worst thing she did was..." He glanced at her, then reluctantly decided to go on. "Okay, this was just before they left for Australia. I had suddenly discovered girls and I had the biggest crush on a pretty older girl named...I don't know, Amanda, I think. She was the sort of girl who wore pink dresses that stuck out all around, and she had her hair in ringlets." He smiled, remembering. "I went dumb and stupid as soon as she showed up anywhere. I wanted to make an impression on her, though. So I used all my allowance and bought her a big red box of candy for Valentine's Day."

"How sweet."

"Yeah. Until she opened it." He threw her a look of pure disgust. "Jalopy found out what I was doing. And just to spite me, she took out all the chocolate truffles and put garden snails in the little slots. When Amanda opened the box, all those little snail heads wiggled at her and she screamed and threw my present up in the air and ran like hell." His eyes mirrored the tragedy. "She never spoke to me again."

Kyra tried to hold back the laughter, but it was difficult. "What is her real name?"

"Jalopy? Jill Clark. May she rot in..."

"Now, now. I think I get the picture."

He grimaced with exasperation. "Aunt Jo doesn't. She keeps saying Jalopy is a changed person. But you notice no one else has wanted to marry her. I'll bet she's exactly the same." A look of quiet satis-

faction came over him at the thought. "Anyway,
Aunt Jo thinks it would be wonderful if the four of
us were back together again. So I could relive the
hell I went through in my childhood."

"The mother is part of the deal?"

"Oh yes. The two of them are coming for a visit
in a couple of weeks. And Aunt Jo is planning the
wedding." His jaw squared with determination.
"You see why I've got to get this taken care of right
away."

She took a long sip of coffee, watching over the
rim of the cup. "Tell me this," she said cheekily.
"What makes you so sure Jalopy will go along with
your aunt's plans? How do you know *she* wants to
marry *you?*"

He shrugged. "She's coming, isn't she?" He put
his napkin up on the table. "Aunt Jo and Jalopy's
mother, Verna, have been cooking this up between
them for years. Believe me, she wouldn't be coming
if she weren't in on it." He looked at her expectantly.
"So, that's settled. I figure Las Vegas would be
quick and clean. We can fly out on Friday and…"

She gazed at him in quiet outrage. "I'm not marrying you," she said firmly.

His bright eyes flickered. "Sure you are. Do you
have anything better to do with the next year of your
life?"

She would have given anything in the world to
have a sharp, quick answer to that one right then.
But she couldn't think of a thing. So she wiped her
mouth with her napkin, put it neatly beside her plate
and rose.

"I'm late for work," she told him, glancing at him

fleetingly as she turned to go. "If I don't watch out, you'll cost me both my jobs."

His grin was endearingly crooked. "No problem. I've got a better job waiting, and you know it."

But she was already striding away, heading for the parking lot. And wondering how in the world she'd gotten herself into such a tangle.

She hurried to her desk only to find the light flashing on her phone. She picked up the receiver and clicked in to her voice mail.

"Hi Kyra," said the cheery voice of Mollie Drew, one of her closest friends from her high school days. "I guess you're not in yet. I've got great news. My brother-in-law, Kevin, is back in town. He had such a fun time last month when I set you two up with the blind date, he wanted me to get you to come over Saturday night. I'll get a babysitter for the kids and we can all go out miniature golfing. Won't that be fun? I'm not going to take no for an answer, kiddo. You need to get out." She paused, made a clicking sound with her tongue, then lowered her voice as though imparting secret information. "Kyra, I know Kevin isn't exactly a dream-boat, but he's got a good job and...well, you know how much your grandmother wants to see you married and settled down. Kevin's a good prospect. Oh, and Kyra...wear something sort of sexy. You always go so conservative. You need to learn to dress to attract a man's attention. You've got so much to offer, you shouldn't keep it hidden. Love ya! Call me!"

Kyra stared at the phone as the message faded away. Her skin was crawling. Kevin was a boring, overbearing geek of a man who had tried to paw her every time she let him near enough. But Mollie was one of her dearest friends. She didn't want to offend her by telling her the truth about her brother-in-law. Like Mollie said, she only wanted what was best for her friend. Kyra stifled the frustrated cry that was trying to claw its way up her throat. Was this what she had to look forward to if she continued following the path she had set? People trying to set her up with geeky men for her own good? Dates with the Kevins of the world? When she *could* be off having a wonderful time with a man like James Redman.

She closed her eyes. No, now she was getting silly. Getting back to work would be a far better thing to do. Gritting her teeth, she sat at her desk and forced herself to think about business.

Still, a delicious thought crept into her brain. Wouldn't it be great to put a message on Mollie's answering machine that said, "Sorry, Mollie. I can't make it on Saturday. I'm afraid I'm going to be too busy. I'm getting married." The thought of it made her smile.

Lunch was a strained situation, no matter how she tried to keep things light. Her friends all seemed to sense there was something going on. But no one wanted to come right out and say anything. Gayle talked about how good her dinner had been the night before at the Rusty Scupper and Chareen told funny stories about how her twins had found a way into a neighbor's yard and climbed a tree and eaten so many barely ripe apricots, she'd been up all night with the resulting upset stomachs. But it was obvious they were all waiting for Kyra to tell them something she wasn't coming up with.

Finally Chareen couldn't stand the suspense any longer and she came right out with what they all were thinking. "Okay, Kyra Symington. If you're not going to volunteer the information, we're going to have to beat it out of you."

Kyra tried to look innocent. "I don't know what you're talking about."

"Cari Parker said you got called in to Mr. Redman's office yesterday. Is that true?"

Kyra knew she was blushing. Just how the heck did you stop that from happening, anyway? "Yes. As a matter of fact, I did."

"Well?" her friends cried in unison. "What happened?"

Only Tracy seemed to think it was unfair to press her. She put a comforting hand on Kyra's arm and said softly, "If you really don't want to talk about it..."

"Don't give her an out!" Chareen cried, throwing out a warning hand. "Come on, girl! Give!"

Kyra looked around at all their expectant faces and knew she had to say something. "He...uh...offered me a job."

Gayle's eyes widened. "Working on the Black Stone Resort development?"

She nodded, but she couldn't meet any of their eyes any longer. There was so much more to it than that.

"Well, are you going to take the job?"

Was she? Was she? "I haven't decided yet," she said. "There are...complications."

The silence at the table was deafening. They were all staring at her. She could feel it. They were wondering what on earth was the matter with her. Funny thing. So was she.

"I would give anything to work on Black Stone," Ann Marie said dreamily.

Kyra looked up and hesitated. She knew from what James had told her that Ann Marie's boss, Kurt Barbour, would soon be working on it, and that meant that Ann Marie would probably be involved. But she had no right to pass on that information at the moment.

"Black Stone is the biggest project this company has ever taken on," Chareen noted dryly. "Any one of us would jump at a chance to work on it."

"Oh, sure," Kyra acknowledged. "So would I. But the job he offered me requires working long hours and some weekends and you know I have my restaurant job to think about."

Chareen rolled her eyes, Ann Marie hiccuped with laughter, but Gayle took her hand and looked earnestly into her face. "Kyra, I know you tend to be as careful and cautious as I do. And you should be careful. But beware of letting safety keep you from living. Sometimes you do have to step outside the predictable and take a chance."

Gayle's intensity obviously came from experience and Kyra took her words as they were meant. "You're right, of course. But how do you know when to be careful and when to risk it all?"

Gayle smiled. "That's why it's called chance. You never know until it's over."

Excited talk about the Black Stone development bubbled up around them and the conversation moved on. But Gayle's words stayed with Kyra. And so did the anguish she'd detected in her friend's eyes. Was she regretting that she had taken a chance—or that she hadn't? Every indication was that the latter was true.

And what chances had Kyra ever taken? When had she ever risked it all to follow a dream? She'd never been much of a gambler, but whatever risk-taking that existed in her character had been asleep ever since that awful day she'd been called home because of the death of her parents. Every step had been supercautious since then, as though she were afraid disaster might be contagious. Was it time to "step outside the predictable," as Gayle had put it? Step out and run. But if so, was James Redman the right one to run to?

Work was impossible. The typed words on pages looked like insects crawling before her eyes. Restlessly, she rose and went into Alice Beals's office to ask about the schedule for the coming week. Alice wasn't there, and as Kyra turned to go, her gaze caught her own name at the top of an open file on Alice's desk. She stopped and looked down at it. "Request for Evaluation" read the heading on the top paper. She knew it was a standard form used when a department requested a transfer or promotion for an employee. Special Projects must have sent it over for Alice to fill out. That didn't bother her at all. What did get her attention was what Alice had already filled in under strengths: "Cautious and dependable."

A surge of righteous anger swept through her. Suddenly that judgment looked less like a commendation and more like a condemnation. Cautious—did that mean "scaredy cat"? Dependable—sure, "She's always around because she's never doing anything interesting." Cautious and dependable. Hah! Cautious and dependable, was she? She'd show the world cautious and dependable!

She was still furious as she rounded the corner on James's office. Pam, his secretary, was typing away on her keyboard and Kyra didn't wait for her to look up. She walked right past the secretary's desk and flung open the door to James's office, hardly noticing Pam's shocked face as she realized what Kyra was doing. And hardly hearing the secretary cry out, "No, wait, Mr. Redman is busy!"

No more cautious. No more dependable. The world was in for a shock.

James was at his desk. He looked up at her in surprise. She strode in and stopped in front of him, her hands on her hips, her eyes flashing. "Okay, buster," she said firmly. "You win. I'll marry you. When's the wedding?"

His handsome face broke into a crooked grin, but his eyes held more amusement than joy. Someone coughed discreetly. Kyra whirled to find Mr. Garlock, director of Budget and Financing and rumored to be in-line for CEO in the not too distant future, standing in front of the bookcase, a bound volume in his hand and a delighted smile on his face.

"Oh," she gasped, then added faintly, "I'm...uh...sorry." She began to back away, her heart fluttering. "I didn't realize...."

"No apologies necessary," Madison Garlock told her, his gray eyes twinkling. He was a tall, handsome man with an air of superiority about him, but a nice light in his gaze. "I'm pleased to be witness to such a charming interchange." He put the book on the shelf and came forward, his hand out. "Let me be the first to offer my congratulations," he said warmly, taking her hand in his and shaking it enthusiastically. "Miss Symington, isn't it? James has been telling me about your whirlwind courtship. I hope you'll be very happy together."

"Th-th-thank you," she managed to stutter, looking at James in astonishment. Why would he have been telling upper management about this crazy scheme? And what, exactly, had he told?

"I'll leave the two of you alone," Madison said smoothly, starting for the door. "I'm sure you have a lot to talk about." He favored James with a knowing grin. "It's always the quiet ones," he told him, as though referring to some inside joke between the two of them. "What did I tell you?" And Kyra suddenly remembered that her sweet, quiet friend Tracy was his administrative assistant. Now what did he mean by that?

But all thoughts of Tracy faded the moment he'd left the room. "What did you tell him?" she asked, eyes wide.

"Just what he needed to know." James was looking her over as though he'd never seen her before. "I had to lay the groundwork. We'll both be taking time off and when we get back, I'll be moving to Contracts. You'll report to Kurt and begin working on Special Projects."

"Oh." That meant her promotion was going through, she supposed. But that hardly seemed important now. And before she could think of anything else, she noticed that James was up out of his chair and coming toward her with a gleam in his eyes that made her take a few steps backward.

"What is going on here?" she demanded.

He grabbed her by the shoulders. "We are getting married," he said with a sensual smile that rendered her breathless. "And I'm going to kiss the bride."

"Oh no you're not," she wanted to say, but somehow never did.

And that might have been because his mouth was covering hers, and his sweet kiss of celebration was quickly becoming something else.

It was her fault, she told herself later when she thought about it. He had meant a simple kiss, a friendly kiss. At least, she thought he had. She was the one who had let her lips part, then taken him in as hungrily as though she'd been starved for a taste of raw masculinity. And maybe that was exactly what it was, because she hadn't been able to stop herself. She'd wanted to feel his tongue slide into her mouth, feel his heat fill her like a shot of brandy on a cold winter's night, feel his hands explore the sensitive parts of her body. In fact, if he hadn't pulled back, she didn't know what might have happened right there in his office. She was lost in a haze of something she didn't want to identify. She hadn't been the one to put a stop to the kiss. Left to her, it might have gone on forever.

It was a sobering realization—that her mind could so easily turn to mush and her body could take over all control, moving on its own without waiting for orders. She was going to have to be more careful in the future.

But wait—wasn't that what she was trying to avoid? Things were becoming too confused. This taking-chances stuff was much scarier than she'd ever dreamed.

But at least she'd done it. She'd made that leap into space. She was sailing out there, arms spread, catching the currents. She closed her eyes and felt the wind in her hair. Her heart thumped in her chest. She was darn proud of herself. She was really flying. Only time would tell if she was going to land on her feet.

Chapter Six

"Aunt Jo?"

"James! You darling boy! It's so good to hear your voice!"

"Hi, Aunt Jo. How are things in Cairo?"

"Things are going swimmingly, darling. My lecture series on the pyramids is getting a lot of local attention. But do you have any idea what time it is here?"

"Oh. Were you asleep? Sorry."

"We *are* on opposite sides of the world."

"I know. I really am sorry. But I had to call and tell you the good news."

"Good news? What good news?"

"I'm getting married."

The pause was too long to mean anything good and he tensed, waiting for her reply. Finally, he couldn't stand the suspense any longer. "Aunt Jo? Did we get cut off? Are you there?"

"I'm here, James. I'm just waiting for the punch line."

"Aunt Jo, this isn't a joke. I'm really getting married."

"Uh-huh. Sure you are. This couldn't have anything to do with the fact that Verna and Jill Clark are arriving to visit us soon, could it?"

"Are they? Gee, I forgot about that."

"Uh-huh. Just the way you'll forget about this engagement of yours as soon as they leave again."

"Why, Aunt Jo! I'm hurt. Are you saying you don't trust me?"

"In anything but love, you're my rock. But the way you spook around marriage talk is a sight to behold, and I think you'd do just about anything to avoid it. I love you, darling, but I'll hold off my congratulations until I see the blushing bride with your ring on her finger."

James grinned. He was anticipating the look on her face when he produced Kyra. It was great to have an antidote to the dread that had cluttered his thinking ever since the spring afternoon when she'd told him what she expected from him. They'd been standing in this very place, the living room of his penthouse apartment, when she'd pointed a bejeweled finger his way and said, "You are going to have to get married."

"Ha! That'll be the day," he'd said, as he always did when the subject of matrimony came up, but at the same time, he'd glanced at his aunt's face and what he'd seen had chilled him. Determination. It was written all over her. And when Aunt Jo was determined, strong men had been known to fold like rows of flimsy party chairs. He'd winced at the sight and turned to look out the wide floor-to-ceiling window that provided a panoramic view of the shoreline, the marina and the ocean beyond. For a moment he'd envied the sailboats heading out toward open sea. He'd rather face Mother Nature any day than Aunt Jo with her game face on.

He could still see her standing there with her hands on her slender hips, her violet-and-silver silk pantsuit shimmering in the sunlight, regarding him with her head tilted, eyes narrowed, as though to say, "Here's something that had better be fixed." He knew that look well. The woman had raised him. No one else had ever loomed so large in his life. And he'd known instinctively that this time, she meant it when she said he'd better get married. And she was ready to do something to make that happen.

Little did he even dream at that time that she would resort to threatening him with Jalopy Clark. But the dread had started that day, just a tiny seed of it. And that was what had finally driven him into offering Kyra a job as his wife. What a crazy world. Or maybe, better said, what a crazy aunt.

He talked to her for a few more minutes, then bid her good-bye and hung up the phone. He didn't have time to chat any longer. His life had changed. He was a busy man. He had a wedding to prepare.

He glanced around his apartment living room, frowning. He was meeting Kyra in half an hour for dinner, after which she was taking him to meet her grandmother. That left a few minutes to think about what he needed to do to get his place ready for a woman to move into. He supposed the cases of beer stacked on the kitchen counter were going to have to go. As well as the girlie calendar the guys at the office had given him for his birthday, which was hanging in the bathroom off the master bedroom. Although there was no hurry there. She probably wouldn't ever go into the bathroom—he was planning to give her the bedroom across the hall that had its own bath—and the Swedish Ice Princess coming up on next month's page was awfully cute, with that little white fur coat opening to show all the best places a man liked to look. He might as well hold off on that one until things got really serious.

In the meantime, he would get the maid who came twice a week to freshen Kyra's bedroom and check to see that she had enough towels and toiletries for her needs. He had no idea what women needed in that department. An awful lot, it always seemed. The maid would know.

And other than that...well, he didn't see why anything else needed changing. The place was great just the way it was.

Feeling pleased with himself for having taken care of that task, he went over a mental checklist. He had his lawyer finishing the contract. His travel agent was booking flights and a room at the Camelot in Las Vegas and making arrangements with a minister in a small chapel that did that sort of thing. And that was about it. He had everything under control. No loose strings that he could see. Nothing to worry about. Everything was settled.

"We have a thousand things that still need to be settled," Kyra told him firmly an hour later as they sat in a cozy booth waiting for dinner in the main dining room at the Friar's Tavern. "Like they say, the devil is in the details."

She frowned at him, not because of what they were talking about, but because he was looking at her as though he would rather nibble on her neck than on the appetizer the waiter had set before them.

"There are a lot of hazards we have to be careful to avoid, you know," she told him tartly. "We've got to be aware of pitfalls."

"Pitfalls?" he asked blankly, his mind still engaged in remembering how she'd melted in his arms earlier that afternoon, how she'd tasted as their kiss had deepened, how her body had fit against his so naturally, how he'd had to pull back before things went too far. How she hadn't really done anything to stop him. "The whole thing is so simple. What could go wrong?"

The evidence of the memories he was enjoying showed in his eyes. She could read his mind as though she were watching a movie. She was going to have to find some way to get this stopped—before he went from PG-13 to an R rating.

"Stop it!" she hissed as she gazed at him in consternation.

"Stop what?" he asked, blinking as though he was coming out of a trance.

"Stop thinking about…you know."

His eyes glinted with amusement. "What are you, the thought police?"

"If I have to be."

He grinned at her, touching her cheek with a crooked finger. "You look cute when you're indignant," he told her.

She would rather look lethal, if only she could manage it. She took a quick drink of ice water, just to calm herself down. Things were moving too quickly. She wished there were more time. A sense of panic kept creeping into her heart. She had the feeling she was just skimming the surfaces of decisions she should be studying in depth.

At least she'd gotten a lot done that afternoon. She'd called Duane Boyd at the Rusty Scupper and told him she was going to have to quit. He'd taken it very well, and she knew there were two other hostesses who had been jockeying for more hours lately, so he wasn't in trouble at all. Still, it was a little sad to have to say good-bye.

She'd cancelled a dental appointment. No regrets there. Taken her white silk suit to a one-hour cleaner. She supposed she would get married in it.

Married! The word shot through her and made her shiver. Was she really going to do this? Could she go through with it? Was she really going to marry this incredibly handsome man sitting beside her—this man she hardly knew? It looked like she was.

She knew she should have taken more time before she'd made her commitment. She should have carefully considered how her actions would impact on everyone around her—especially her grandmother.

The last thing she'd done before she left the house was to tell her grandmother about her plans. It had been hard to do, and she ached from having done it. She'd told her grandmother a lie. The guilt cut her like a knife. She hated lying. There was no use telling herself it was all for the best, because that hadn't been proved yet. Telling her grandmother a lie was an awful thing to do, even if it was for her own good. Deep down, she couldn't help but believe that she would pay for it, somehow.

Her grandmother had been surprised—but de-

lighted. The suddenness of it didn't seem to bother
her at all. She only wanted to know when she would
get to meet the groom, and Kyra had promised to
bring him by after dinner.

She still hadn't settled with Nurse O'Brien about
her mother's care while she was gone to Las Vegas.
They would have to discuss it after dinner, when she
took James home to introduce him. That was the
largest burden weighing on her at the moment. Car-
ing for her grandmother was the most important
thing.

The waiter appeared with a cart from which he
produced a covered plate that he presented to Kyra,
and another which he put down in front of James.
The covers were removed to reveal two thick cuts of
prime rib flanked with asparagus spears and golden
puffs of Yorkshire pudding. The meal looked beautiful, but one glance and Kyra's stomach told her she
wasn't going to be eating a thing. She sighed. Oh
well, if she couldn't eat, she might as well talk. As
she'd warned him a few minutes before, there was
still a lot to settle.

"Okay, here's something that could be a problem," she said, trying to stick to the issue at hand.
This was fundamental and she wanted to get it out
in the open where it could be dealt with—and hopefully put to rest. "What if…if you decide you like
me too much?"

His eyebrows rose quizzically. "What do you
mean?"

She took a deep breath and contemplated another
gulp of water.

"I mean, I thought we'd agreed that this was not
going to be a…a sexual arrangement."

"No, of course not." But a slow smile was beginning to curl the corners of his wide mouth. "Unless, of course, we both decide…"

"No!" She flushed. That had come out a little louder than she'd expected. But she meant it. "No," she said, more softly, but with just as much intensity. "That is something we have to get straight from the first. What I've agreed to is a business arrangement, pure and simple. If you try to turn it into anything else, I'll have to leave."

His turquoise eyes clouded. He didn't understand what the big deal was. A little sex would only add to the experience as far as he was concerned. It wasn't as though she weren't interested. If she tried to sell that one to him, he would have to prove her wrong. And he knew after the kiss they'd shared that afternoon that proving her wrong would be perfectly easy, no matter how she denied it. A part of him resented her attitude.

"Don't worry," he said smoothly. "It won't have to come to that. After all, I've got other resources." His bright gaze challenged hers as he shrugged. "If I feel the need for something like that—"

"Not while we're married." She said it firmly, with conviction. She wasn't asking, she was telling.

He blinked again, surprised. He hadn't really thought that through, and now that he was beginning to face reality, he realized there was going to be more to this marriage thing than he'd supposed. "Oh. No, I guess that wouldn't work, would it?"

"Of course not."

He frowned. "But wait—"

"No, you wait." She jabbed a finger in his chest. She was getting braver and braver. "If you want this business arrangement, I have a few requirements of my own and I want them addressed in the contract.'' She pulled out a piece of carefully folded paper and handed it to him. ''Here are a few things I wrote down while I was waiting for you.''

He flipped open the page and scanned it quickly. ''What, no clothing allowance? No breakfast trays brought to you in bed every morning?'' His smile was teasing. ''These seem perfectly reasonable. I'll hand them over to my lawyer.'' He tucked the paper into his breast pocket. ''Which reminds me. You ought to have someone look over the contract on your part before you sign it.''

''I will. I know someone I can call.''

''Good.''

''Okay, here's something else,'' she said, ignoring the twitch at the corner of his mouth that might have been hinting at annoyance on his part. ''I know you're talking about going to Las Vegas to get married. Well, I've got mixed feelings about that.''

He grinned. ''Who doesn't?''

''What I mean is, I was thinking it might hurt my grandmother to be left out of things. I mean, if I were really getting married, I would certainly include her in the ceremony.''

He shrugged. ''You want to take her along?''

''No.'' A giggle bubbled up her throat at the thought of her grandmother in Las Vegas. ''No, that's not it at all. I explained to her that you are very busy with this new Black Stone project and that we have to go to Las Vegas because we can get the legalities taken care of more quickly. She was very understanding. And Nurse O'Brien pointed out that she is really too ill to be anywhere near a wedding. Even a ceremony in her bedroom would probably be too much for her to handle.''

He frowned. ''Is she really that sick?''

Kyra hesitated, then nodded. ''All I ask is that we do something for her when we get back. A little candlelight ritual at her bedside or something. Just to make her feel included.'' She searched his face. Was he going to allow her this?

He shrugged again. ''Sure,'' he said carelessly. ''Whatever you think. You arrange it and tell me where to stand.''

He hates having to do it, she told herself, watching him. Well, that was just the way most men were. She was going to have to find ways to work around it. ''Thank you,'' she said crisply, taking another drink of water.

He watched her for a moment, enjoying the way her throat moved as she drank. In fact, he was enjoying more and more about this woman. Then he remembered something and he patted absently at one pocket, then another, reaching in to retrieve a small velvet bag.

''One more thing,'' he told her. ''I guess you'd better have a ring.'' He pulled the bag open and shook out a diamond ring into his hand. ''Hope it fits,'' he muttered, reaching for her hand. He slid it onto her ring finger. It fit perfectly.

She stared at it. It was beautiful, a large, brilliant stone in a marquise cut and an old-fashioned setting. The facets caught the light and scattered flashes around the area like glittering confetti. ''Oh,'' she gasped, almost blinded by the sparkle. And then for a moment, nothing else would come out. Something was blocking her throat.

"It was my grandmother's," he said casually. "So I'll have to ask for it back once the year is over. But, unless you hate it..."

"Oh. Oh, no!" She started to pull it off. "Oh, I can't wear your grandmother's ring!"

"Why not?" He covered her hand with his own, stopping her. "If you don't, nobody ever will. I'm certainly not planning to do this again."

She looked down at his large, strong hand, at the diamond glittering between his fingers, at her own pale skin, and her eyes filled with tears. Chances were good that she wouldn't ever do this again, either. This was it. And the ring was so beautiful. If only... A fat, hot tear dropped onto James's hand.

"Hey." He lifted her chin to look into her eyes and found them brimming. He looked startled, then a smile began to curl his lips. "I know what's wrong," he said softly in a lightly teasing voice. "You're thinking about what a nice ring your accordion player might have offered, aren't you? Something in orange plastic, perhaps?"

She smiled through her tears, nodding and biting her lip so that it wouldn't tremble. "With a tiny squirt bottle attached, like in the comics," she said when she was under enough control to talk. And then she laughed softly.

He smiled back, then bent forward and kissed her lips in a soft, comforting gesture that made her gasp, but only lasted seconds.

"Let's eat," he said, turning back to the food. "We're going to need to build our strength. We've got a long weekend ahead of us."

She made some attempts at eating, stabbing at her

food and moving it around the plate. But she kept looking at the ring. It looked darn good on her hand.

Driving in to work the next morning, Kyra turned on her car radio and found the song "Crazy" playing. That made her laugh. It could be her theme song. What in the world was she doing? She felt a little like a leaf caught in a fast-moving river. A chain of events had been set in motion and now it looked as though nothing could stop it.

James had come to her house to meet her grandmother the night before. She'd been a little nervous. Her house was so small, so modest, what would he think? But she had to admit, he'd been completely natural. And her grandmother had loved him, as he bent over her and took her hand in his and talked to her with that overwhelmingly seductive smile of his. Even Nurse O'Brien had been charmed. She had a feeling they would bundle her up and hand her over to him if she decided to back out of the wedding at the last minute.

Arriving at her desk, she found a message waiting. Kurt Barbour wanted to see her in his office as soon as possible. Things were moving so quickly, she was going to fall behind if she didn't watch out. She took a deep breath and marched down the hall. Ann Marie was just taking the cover off her computer and she turned and stared as Kyra passed her with a wink and went right in to Mr. Barbour's office.

"You asked to see me?" she said.

Kurt turned and rose to greet her, smiling. "Sit," he said, gesturing toward the chair on the other side of the desk. "I know you're leaving for a very special long weekend this afternoon and I thought we should talk before you go.''

''Yes?'' she said, acting noncommittal, but certain of what he was up to. He wanted to look her over, no doubt. He wanted to see what the heck James was getting himself into. He looked friendly enough, but she had a feeling he was thinking, *What on earth is James doing marrying this dowdy little office worker? Has he gone insane?*

''I understand we'll be working together soon,'' he went on. ''I know you haven't been officially notified, so I won't congratulate you just yet, but I've been looking over your file and I want to let you know I'll be very happy to have you working on my team when I take over Special Projects.''

''Oh.'' She knew she was flushing, both with embarrassment and pleasure. ''I'm looking forward to it.''

''Good.'' He frowned, looking down at papers on his desk. ''I must say, looking at the recommendations and the evaluations of your work, I don't know why you haven't been promoted before this. There seems to be universal admiration for the job you do here.''

''Thank you, sir. I guess I've never really gone after any openings before.'' Nor was she ever encouraged to. She was beginning to wonder if she should have been a little more aggressive. Maybe she hadn't had the urge because she'd always been too tired from her second job.

''Well,'' he went on, ''now that you and James are getting married, of course...''

Of course. He let the sentence hang there, but she thought she knew what he meant. If she were going to be James's wife, she would need a job with better standing. Well, she couldn't argue with that. But it made her realize just how odd this was going to look to everyone once they got wind of it. Rumors would, undoubtedly, fly. Everyone would be counting the months to see if she was pregnant. She hated this. She wasn't wild about being the subject of rumors to begin with, but rumors like this...

"At any rate, I'm glad we've met."

She took that as her cue to rise and shake his hand before turning toward the door.

"Let me caution you," he added, following her to the door. "The announcement of your promotion won't be made until this afternoon. Please don't mention any of this to anyone until then."

She turned to look at him, her head to the side. "Ann Marie, your secretary, is a good friend of mine. Does she know?"

"No, she doesn't know a thing about it yet." He grinned at her. "Don't tell her why I asked you here. It'll drive her crazy."

Kyra's smile lighted up her face and showed Kurt evidence to explain James's fascination. "Are you sure you can hold out against Ann Marie on a tear?" she said.

"No," he admitted, laughing. "But it will be fun trying."

She laughed, too. The spark of humor in his eyes was contagious. She had a feeling they would get along fine working side by side. As she left, she gave Ann Marie a smug smile and hurried away, ignoring the look of curious outrage on her friend's face.

"What's this?" Chareen picked up the long-stemmed rose that had been left at her place at the table and narrowed her eyes, watching Kyra. "Okay, lady of mystery. Don't you think it's about time you let the old gang in on what the hell is going on?"

Kyra nodded. She'd put a rose at each place because she wanted to include her friends somehow. This was a celebration. Suddenly she felt as though she had a balloon inside her, and someone was busy pumping it up. She was going to float away any minute. She'd better get this over with in a hurry. She took a long look around the table at each one of her friends.

"I'm just about to leave for the weekend. A long weekend. I'll be back Wednesday. But I had to tell you all before I left—"

"But where are you going?" Ann Marie asked accusingly, her violet eyes stormy. "You never said anything about a weekend trip!"

"I know. I've kept this from you, and I wish I hadn't had to. But now I want to tell you all about it."

They each sat silently, staring at her with wide eyes. There wasn't a sound around the table. She looked at each friend in turn, and felt a surge of love for them all.

"I'm getting married," she blurted out at last. "I'm marrying James Redman. In Las Vegas." They were still staring, each and every mouth slightly open. "This weekend," she added, just for emphasis. "I wish I could invite you all, but this was so sudden—"

"I'll say it's sudden," Chareen said, skepticism crackling in her eyes. "Is this some kind of joke? Are you trying to get our goat?"

"No." Kyra began to laugh. "No, not at all."

"You really expect us to believe you're marrying a man you could barely speak to three days ago?" Gayle challenged, a frown on her pretty face. "Come on, Kyra. What's this all about?"

"I'm getting married," Kyra said, still laughing as she rose from the table and looked down at them. "I'm sorry it seems so strange. Believe me, it's strange to me, too, but…"

"Oh, Kyra, do you think maybe you've been working too hard?" Tracy asked sympathetically, looking worried for her. "Sometimes when you're under a lot of stress and get too tired, you can think things are happening that aren't really happening at all."

Kyra shook her head, looking at them and laughing aloud. What could she do to convince them?

"Look," Tracy said, grabbing her hand and holding it up. "A ring!"

They all gasped and crowded around, oohing and aahing over the ring on her finger.

"You see?" she said. "This is for real. Really."

They didn't seem to want to believe it despite the ring. But it didn't matter, because all of a sudden, James was there.

"Good afternoon, ladies," he said, smiling at them all. "I'm afraid I'm going to have to steal Kyra away from you. We have a plane to catch." He looked at Kyra and dropped a quick kiss on her temple. "Shall we go?"

"Yes." She gave him a radiant smile, then looked back at her friends. "Goodbye. I'll see you next week," she told them.

Not one of them had the self-possession to say a word. And as they left the cafeteria, James and Kyra were holding hands and smiling into each other's eyes. Just as though it were real.

Chapter Seven

Las Vegas lay below like a shimmering jewel in the dark desert night. Kyra pressed closer to the window, wanting to see it all. James watched her, enjoying her excitement. Sometimes she seemed so open, as though she had no sense of self-consciousness at all. When that happened, he felt like he could see into her heart and soul. And then a minute later her wariness would come back over her in a wave, and she would close him out again. He was beginning to hate that wall that came between them. He wanted to see what she was thinking. When the wall came down, her face didn't allow anything to escape. He wished he knew what she was so afraid of.

The airport was swarming with travelers from all over the world and all over the map, culturally. They had to push their way to the baggage area, but they got their luggage quickly enough and went to flag down a cab. Kyra saw a familiar-looking woman and grabbed James's arm.

"Isn't that…? Oh, but she's dead. It can't be!"

James grinned. "It's not. And yet it is." He winked at her. "It's a look-alike. Las Vegas is crawling with them these days. There's a big show at the C'est la Vie. They've got Humphrey Bogart and Clark Gable and Buster Keaton. Maybe we'll try to catch it."

The cab came and Kyra snuck one more look at the look-alike before she climbed in ahead of James. The hotel was only a short distance from the airport, one of the farthest out on the Strip, but James had the driver take them farther in to town, past the chapel where the ceremony was going to be held the next day.

"It's called The Little Chapel of Love," James told him.

"Sure, I know it," the driver said, and a few minutes later he slowed. "There she is," he called back to them.

Kyra looked out, telling herself not to care about it. It didn't mean a thing. They weren't going to have a real marriage, so this wasn't a real wedding. But she was disappointed all the same.

She stared at the little pink lump of a building. Paint was peeling off the stucco walls, showing that the previous paint job had been a neon purple. The sign out front was flashing on and off. No Waiting, it read. Weddings Done in Your Car. A pair of scraggly little plants lined the walkway. Faded plastic flowers were stuck in them. All in all, a more depressing sight would be hard to conjure.

Neither of them said anything as the driver made a U-turn and headed back toward the hotel. What was there to say? It only had to be utilitarian, nothing more.

The hotel was a relief after the chapel. They drove up the long, sweeping driveway lined with a hundred thousand gold-and-silver lights, turning nighttime into day. A doorman dressed like a medieval castle guard helped them out of the cab and into the lobby.

"The Camelot," Kyra murmured breathlessly. "I've always wanted to come inside and see what it was really like."

"Why didn't you?" he asked casually.

She looked at him sideways. Didn't he know? The Camelot was the swankiest place in town. When she'd visited Las Vegas, she'd stayed at more family-oriented hotels, closer in toward the center of town. The Camelot always seemed to be out on its own, a sort of fantasyland for rich people.

And it was lovely. The walls were royal-red brocade edged in gold, with granite pillars interspersed here and there, giving the place an ancient look. The carpet was so thick, she was afraid she might sink and get lost in it. They had to cross a moat filled with swans to get from the check-in desk to the main lobby. The elevator was a castle tower room that moved. And when they were escorted to their suite, they found themselves in a room the size of a small auditorium, lined with tapestries, and with a canopy bed that could have honored King Arthur himself.

"Especially if he was about six-foot-ten," James noted when she told him what she was thinking. "Are you sure you didn't give us the room for visiting basketball teams by mistake?" he asked the bellhop, who grinned and ducked his head and reached for the tip James was holding out.

He turned and looked at Kyra as the young man left the room. "Well, how do you like it?" he asked, though he could see her answer in her shining eyes.

"It's wonderful," she said, turning slowly to take it all in. "I feel like a princess. This really is made to seem like a castle."

"Better than a castle. At least we have running water and electricity instead of candles."

She laughed. "You're right. Better than a castle." She looked toward the door at the far end of the room and then at the large bed. "Where do I sleep?"

For some reason, her asking that took all the wind out of his sails. It didn't make any sense that it should bother him. After all, he knew they were only playacting this marriage thing. And he'd never really wanted to marry anyway. But when she put it so blatantly, as though reminding him not to get too close or too carried away, it put his back up, and he frowned and growled as he answered.

"There's another bed in the next room." He pointed out the side door that led to one of the three rooms that comprised their suite. "Don't worry. I won't forget our contract."

She flashed him a smile, as though she didn't catch the undertone of resentment at all. "Great. I'll go put my things away."

He watched her go and sank onto the couch, brooding. All the preparations and the rushing to make the plane had kept him from thinking too much about what they were doing there in Vegas. But it was finally catching up with him. He was getting married. He'd thought he would never do such a thing. It was no wonder he felt a vague sense of anger.

That was it. That had to be it. He was edgy because he was about to do something he'd always sworn he would never do. He'd seen marriages that worked and marriages that didn't, but he'd never seen a marriage where the man wasn't trapped like an animal in a cage, forced to live according to some woman's idea of what life was supposed to be like. Something about the way Kyra had asked where she was going to sleep had brought that back to him in full force. He could set up all the rules he wanted. He could post the contract on the wall. He could spend all his time at the office. It wouldn't stop the inevitable from happening. She was going to change the way he lived his life. She was going to be a wife.

He groaned and told himself to grow up. It was only for a year. He could stand anything for a year. Maybe he would put up one of those calendars that show every month at once and mark off the days. But no. He had a feeling she might resent that.

See? There she went, affecting his life again! He hated that.

"Let's go eat," he said to her impatiently when she came out of the side room. "We can finish the unpacking later."

She hesitated, wondering if her plain linen dress was too wrinkled from the flight to wear to a dining room. But James didn't sound as though he would relish waiting while she changed. And he was the boss, wasn't he? So she laid aside her misgivings and grabbed her purse so that she could catch up with him before he got to the elevator. He was silent as he escorted her through the casino. Lights flashed and music played and the dealers cracked jokes at the blackjack tables. There was too much to see. They hurried by so fast, it seemed a bright, neon blur.

He led her to the far side of the building and through a doorway that seemed nondescript. And suddenly they were in a dining room that was obviously exclusive and not for the general public. They were shown to a table immediately by a man who spoke in French and wore a stunning tuxedo. Kyra sat in a huge upholstered chair and felt like a little girl whose feet didn't reach the floor. Two waiters lifted her chair and put her in the proper position at the damask-covered table. She felt like giggling but she managed to hold it back, and it faded completely once she'd looked at James's face and saw he was finding nothing amusing at the moment.

They didn't have to order. Food was brought to them without a word being said. The delicacies that appeared were beautiful and tasty, but she couldn't name a thing she saw. Most were cut into elegant shapes and dipped in fancy sauces, and looked like food a continental princess might eat. She tried a little bit of everything, completely delighted. But her appetite waned when she noticed James was nursing his drink and not eating anything at all. She had no idea what was bothering him, but she could see that he wasn't in the mood for a little light conversation, so she left him alone. And that was when she began to study their surroundings.

At first it was difficult to get a good look at any of their fellow diners. Each was in a chair just as large as the ones she and James sat in, so that most of them were hidden from view. But if she watched long enough, someone would peek around the back of a chair or lean forward to take a bit of food from a serving tray, and suddenly be visible. She frowned, because she thought she'd seen some strangely familiar faces. Were they more look-alikes? Or the real thing? But James didn't look approachable and still hadn't said a word, so she kept the puzzle to herself for the time being.

Then an extremely elegant older couple stopped by their table to say hello.

"James, my dear fellow," said the gentleman in a clipped British accent. "So good to see you."

"Sir Randolph!" James was suddenly all smiles, rising from his chair to shake hands with Sir Randolph and then to actually kiss the hand of the lady who accompanied him, making Kyra raise an eyebrow. "I'd heard you were still in Switzerland."

"No, no. Couldn't take the racket. All that singing." The man shook his head disapprovingly and James looked questioningly at his lady.

"We were stranded in a hotel full of German tourists," she told him with a lovely laugh. "They waved their beer steins and sang drinking songs all day. We had to escape on the first available flight, and it brought us straight here."

James grinned. "A likely story," he said, then turned to introduce the couple to Kyra.

They were pleasant enough, but Kyra saw the dismissal in their eyes. At first she wasn't sure why. Did they think she was just some bimbo? James hadn't mentioned that they were going to be married the next day. Or was it something else? She listened as they exchanged more pleasantries and urged James to join them for baccarat that evening—without, she noticed, mentioning her—before taking their leave. And in the meantime, she thought she'd seen a famous face at another table.

"Isn't that...?" she began when James sat.

"Yes, it is," he told her, and nodded to the man, who nodded back and gave a little wave.

"You know him?" she whispered, eyes wide.

"Sure." He looked at her absently. "He spends a lot of time in France between films and I met him there one summer when I was in college."

"Oh."

He noticed her consternation and decided to explain. "Look, I don't know if I told you, but my Aunt Jo is a world-famous archeologist. She gets invited to all kinds of festivals and exhibits and meets famous people wherever she goes. She pretty much put her career in abeyance while she was raising me, but when I turned sixteen, she started up again and took me along to digs and lectures and everything else she was going to, as long as I wasn't in school. I became friendly with all her friends." He shrugged. "It's funny, but the same group of people seem to turn up in the same places all over the world. And one of those places is here, at the Camelot. I've been here so often over the years, it sometimes feels like a high-school reunion every time I show up."

"I see." She felt even smaller in her great big chair.

His life was such a contrast to hers. She'd never met anyone she'd become friendly with in that way but the local branch librarian and the swim instructor at her neighborhood Y. It was exciting to be there, but she was beginning to wonder why she'd been his choice to share this with him. She really didn't fit in, and it seemed to be obvious to everyone but James.

A group of young women stopped by to flirt with James, and he flirted right back. They hardly gave Kyra a second glance and she felt ignored, until James made a point of introducing her. Then they were overly sweet and she couldn't help but be a little cool in response.

"Is it my imagination," James asked as they left, "or did the temperature just go down ten degrees in here?"

She flashed him a look and went back to her dessert. She might feel out of place, dowdy and horribly underdressed, but she wasn't about to slink off with her tail between her legs. Still, there was no doubt she was beginning to feel miserable.

They rose to leave just as a silver-haired woman in a mauve silk suit turned and caught sight of James. She hurried over, kissed him on both cheeks and insisted he must have a drink with her that evening. Kyra waited while they talked. The woman's clothes reeked of money. As a matter of fact, everyone else in the room had that same well-tailored look, even one young woman who barely wore anything at all. You only got that look by shopping at the very highest end of the retail market. Or having your clothes made for you by a very expensive designer. Kyra felt like a scullery maid standing there in the middle of the room where everyone could see her.

Someone else called to James from a nearby table and he turned to say something to him. The silver-haired woman glanced at Kyra, looked her up and down, taking in the rumpled linen dress that had been a bargain at Macy's, and dismissed her with an audible sniff, starting to turn away.

"Oh, you poor thing," Kyra said, her eyes shooting daggers. "I see you have a cold. Here, have a tissue." She dug into her pocket and grabbed a clean but rumpled tissue she'd carried all day and thrust it into the woman's hand. "You wouldn't want to spread your germs to all these nice people, now would you?" she said in a loud, cheerful voice.

The woman held the tissue as though it were a rat that might leave droppings on her. Her carefully painted mouth was contorted with horror. Kyra turned, smiling fiercely, and marched resolutely toward the exit with James, who'd turned back in time to catch their exchange, coming close behind.

She was sure he was furious with her. The woman was probably someone very important. But she didn't care. She was sick and tired of being treated like James's poor relation.

"I'm sorry," she told him, still not looking him in the face as they got into the elevator. "I just couldn't take being snubbed by your friends one more time."

He didn't say a word and she finally looked up in trepidation, only to find him laughing silently, his eyes dancing as they met hers.

"You're not angry?" she said, relieved.

He shook his head. "No," he said, his voice husky from trying to hold back his laughter. "I never saw anything so funny in my life," he told her. "I'll bet she soaks her hand in bleach tonight."

She looked into his eyes and smiled, and for a moment, there was an electricity between them that couldn't be denied. But then the elevator came to a stop and the doors opened and they had to get out.

The room seemed strangely quiet as they entered. James glanced at the clock. It was still too early to go to bed. Besides, they should be celebrating. They were getting married tomorrow. He turned to look at Kyra. She looked at him. The wariness was there. How was he going to get her to drop her guard?

One thing was sure, they couldn't sit there and stare at each other for the next two hours. He frowned, turning slowly to see what she was doing, and found her watching him.

"Are you going down to join your friends?" she asked him, pushing her hair back behind her ear.

He stared at her for a long moment before answering. He'd forgotten all about that. "Do you want me to?" he asked.

She shrugged. "I...I don't care. I've got a magazine to read. You can do whatever you like."

He took a step toward her, then another, reaching out to touch her soft, beautiful hair. "Don't you want to spend the night before our wedding together?" he said softly.

Her eyes widened and for just a moment, he thought he saw something...but no. The wall was there, keeping him from her thoughts. His hand sank into her hair, cupping the back of her head. Suddenly he needed a reaction from her, something real, something genuine. He bent to kiss her and she tried to pull away, but he wouldn't let her. His mouth covered hers and her resistance melted. She tasted so good, like summer, like sunshine, like a woman with loving on her mind. And it was certainly on his.

He wanted her. Her tongue touched his and it was as though a dam had broken and heat poured through him, and he wanted her more than he'd wanted any other woman in a long, long time. He pulled her close, crushing her against his hard body, and felt her mold against him. He was taking her for his own the next day, laying a claim. He wanted to make it real this night.

But she was pulling away again. He didn't want to let her go, and he tightened his hold, deepening the kiss, pulling her into the cradle of his hips so that she would know....

"James," she gasped out. "No!"

He stopped dead, letting her break away from him. She stared at him, her hand to her mouth, her eyes wide and wary. He stared back, his jaw hardening, the vein at his temple pulsing. She didn't have to speak. He knew what she was thinking, knew it included words like "contract" and "business deal." He knew he was wrong to try to turn this into something more. But for some irrational reason, there was a slow, smoldering anger inside him. He wasn't used to being rejected. Maybe that was it. Whatever it was, he knew he had better get out before he did something really stupid. Without a word, he turned and headed for the door.

Kyra lay in her bed and stared at the lights flashing into her window from somewhere across the street. He'd been gone for over an hour. Her insides were churning.

What was she going to do? If she had any sense at all, she would be on a plane flying back home. How could she marry a man she couldn't resist?

That might seem odd, but in this case it was a dangerous truth. Every time he kissed her, she went weak in the knees and began riding imaginary merry-go-rounds. She hadn't had a lot of experience with sex. She'd gone to bed with Gary twice. No bells had rung. No angels had sung. She didn't hear a symphony. And shortly after, he'd dumped her.

But this was different. She could tell, because this time, her body was making a clear cry for satisfaction. And satisfaction meant having James take her and fill her with his strength. She felt restless, achy, desperate for his touch. Suddenly, she realized she now knew what they meant when they spoke of hungering for a man. How was she going to go through a year of this? She couldn't imagine.

It wasn't supposed to be this way. The contract was supposed to protect them. Strictly business—that was their relationship. That was what they'd sworn to make it. It hadn't really even begun, and already she was having grave doubts that they could pull it off.

If she was honest, she would have to admit that deep in her heart of hearts, she had dreams. She had her own fantasies about what might happen, about how he might look at her one day and think, "Say, this isn't so bad. Maybe we should make it permanent." To be married to James Redman—really married—not this pretend thing. She had to admit, the fantasy had its appealing aspects.

But it was time to get back to reality. She was hired help. The prince didn't marry the maid. The boss didn't marry the copy girl. Not that she was actually a copy girl. Still, it made the point. She and James were business partners. She wasn't from his world and she never could be.

Besides, there was more to it than that. She didn't want to feel this way about him. She definitely didn't want to fall in love. Falling in love left you vulnerable. She knew that from watching the world around her and she knew it from experience. When you fell in love with a man, you started to depend on him. Then, just when you needed him most, he was sure to disappear. Her father had never been there for her mother. Whenever a crisis arose, he managed to be someplace else. Then Gary had done the same to her. When she'd reached out to him, he'd evaporated. She'd learned that the best defense was never getting yourself in the position to need anyone.

She was not, repeat, not, going to fall in love with James.

But she couldn't lie there waiting for him to show up any longer either. She was going to go looking for him. Bounding out of bed, she headed for the bathroom and ran a comb through her hair, then pulled a tunic and pants set out of the closet and slipped into them. In no time at all, she was on the floor of the casino, searching. James was nowhere to be found.

"May I help you?" a voice asked. "You look a bit lost."

She turned to find a small gray-haired woman smiling at her from behind an open Dutch door. "Oh, uh, who are you?" Kyra asked, realizing she must have some official capacity, but having no clue what that might be.

"I'm Mrs. Denigrew, the concierge. My job is to help in any way I can."

"Oh. Well…I'm looking for my, uh, fiancé. He said he might play baccarat. Do you have any idea where he might be?"

"Of course. Follow me." The woman came out from behind her partition and led Kyra to a set of double doors that were slightly ajar. "You'll find him in here, my dear. Let me know if I can be of any further use.''

Kyra looked in, and there he was in a velvet-draped side room, playing the elegant game with five or six men and women, each of them looking more golden than the next. She stood in the doorway and watched for a few minutes. No one noticed her. And no one would have done anything but frown at her if they had. She didn't belong with them. She could see that very clearly. James was from an alien place, and he was of an alien species. How could she ever hope to make a niche for herself in his world, even temporarily?

He turned and saw her, but it was too late. She'd seen all she needed to see. She left the room, walking deliberately across the floor and then around the perimeter of the casino. She looked back. He wasn't following her. That had been her last hope. Despairing, she turned into a darkened lounge and sat at a table in the back. The room was not large. Thirty or thirty-five tables were crowded into it, most of them taken by parties of three or four. A girl in a cowboy hat was on stage, singing her heart out about love lost, love found, love discarded along the way. She wondered, fleetingly, what the ratio was between happy love songs and sad ones. She had a feeling the happy ones were hard to find.

"One Shirley Temple," she told the waitress. "Wait. Make that a double."

"Two cherries, you mean?" the waitress asked, just to be sure.

Kyra nodded. She needed something to cheer her up.

It came in a tall, silvery glass. She dug for one of

the cherries and ate it, savoring the sweet taste, but feeling as though her world was collapsing.

"Are you lonesome tonight?" a deep voice asked her.

She turned and squinted in the dim light. "Elvis?" she asked, incredulous.

"Yes, ma'am. You don't know me. But I'd sure like to join you, if I may."

"Sure. Of course." She watched as the tall man dressed in a white, bell-bottomed jumpsuit accented by a massive, studded belt pulled up a chair and planted himself in it. His thick dark hair was swept back in a pompadour, and large sunglasses hid his eyes, even though it was barely light enough to see anything in this dimly lighted room. He looked so much like the King. Of course, he couldn't be, but still. "My name is Kyra," she said, shaking hands with the man. "How are you?"

"I'm fine, Kyra, but you look like a Heartbreak Hotel reject."

"I do?" She didn't want it to be that obvious.

"Yes, you do. I had to come by, just because I saw you over here, lookin' like you were about to sit right down and cry. I had to see if you would let me do somethin' to cheer you up."

"That's nice of you." She gave him a bittersweet smile. "Maybe you could sing me a song."

"I'd like to, sugar, but I can't rightly compete with the lady on stage right now. It wouldn't be polite." He gestured toward the girl in the cowboy hat. "But I've got a good shoulder. You can cry like a baby on it if you want."

"Oh." The thought of crying on Elvis's shoulder was a kick. "No, I don't think—"

"Come on, baby. I gotta know. What's got you all shook up?"

She studied him carefully. He seemed genuinely concerned. And he *was* Elvis. "Well, the fact is, I'm getting married tomorrow."

"Hey, that's all right, Mama," he said, smiling. "I'm happy for you."

She laughed softly, shaking her head. "Do you always do that?" she asked him.

"Do what?" He cocked his head, waiting.

"You know, use Elvis song titles in everything you say. I swear I've caught at least five of them so far."

He looked puzzled. "Sorry, Miss Kyra. I don't know what you're talking about."

"Oh." She hid a smile. "Okay."

"And you're avoiding the issue. I don't have much time. It's now or never. So tell me, what's so scary about getting married tomorrow?"

"Well, you see, we don't really love each other." She couldn't believe this. She was telling her secrets to the King, confiding in a stranger. But then, how could Elvis really be a stranger? "And I'm not sure this is the right thing to do."

He nodded sagely. "That could be a problem. After all, sugar, without love, there is nothing."

"That's what I'm afraid of." She leaned a little closer, bemused but game. It felt good to finally be able to talk to someone. She hadn't realized how much that had been bothering her. "We're doing it for reasons I can't really explain, but it will benefit us both. Still, I don't know. What do you think? Should I go through with it?"

"Hmm." He thought over her problem, treating it

quite seriously. Someone stuck a head around the barrier and called to him softly.

"Elvis! Come on, man. You're on next."

He raised a hand. "Hold on a minute, Scotty," he told the intruder, then turned back to her. "Don't ask me why, but I'm getting a real strong feeling about this. I think you're afraid you're beginning to like this fella too much, and that's trouble. There's nothing sadder than a one-sided love affair. But honey, I think you ought to consider this. They say the most happy marriages are those arranged by others. People who live together can learn to love. It happens all the time. I think he'll end up loving you real soon."

"You do?"

"Sure." He rose, then took her hand and kissed it. "Treat him nice. Your wish will come true. Come on, now. I'm countin' on you."

And he was gone as suddenly as he'd appeared.

Kyra felt a giggle coming up her throat. She'd just been sitting there asking Elvis for love advice. How nuts was that? But when you came right down to it, who knew more about love than the man who spent his life singing about it?

"*Here* you are."

She looked up quickly to find James standing in the light from outside the lounge.

"I've been searching the whole damn place for the past half hour," he said, sinking into the seat Elvis had just vacated. He'd brought along a drink in a tall glass, and he took a sip of it before he set it down.

"I've been right here all that time," she told him serenely. And she smiled. *Treat him nice,* Elvis had advised.

He stared at her smile as though he didn't quite

believe in it. She reached out and took his hand. His fingers curled around hers. "Why didn't you come into the baccarat pit?" he asked.

Her smile faltered. How could she explain a thing like that to him? "Why didn't you follow me out?" she asked in turn.

"I tried," he told her. "But an old, old, old friend of my aunt's pulled me over to meet someone and by the time I could get away, you were gone with the wind."

He took another drink from his glass with a flourish and she realized he'd had more than he should have. He was holding himself just a little too stiffly, and his words were ever so slightly slurred.

"You're sloshed," she said accusingly.

"I am…I am not," he declared, looking as innocent as a newborn lamb. "I never drink too much. I know exactly how to…how to…" His handsome brow furrowed with puzzlement. "What was the question?"

She would have told him, but at that moment, applause drew her attention and she realized her Elvis friend had taken the stage.

"Look," she whispered to James. "It's Elvis."

He squinted at the stage. "Can't be," he said. "He's dead."

The man on stage didn't seem to know that. He took the applause as his due, bowing to right and left, then took the microphone in his hand.

"Thank you. Thank you. I'd like to start tonight with a favorite of mine, 'Can't Help Falling in Love.' And I'd like to dedicate it to a friend out in the audience who's getting married tomorrow. Good luck to you, Kyra, darlin'."

Kyra laughed softly and threw him a kiss. James took another sip of his drink and looked as though he might slip right off the chair. The song began.

"Hey," James said blearily. "It sure does sound like Elvis."

She looked at him and shook her head. "You are a mess," she told him, but there was more affection than criticism in her tone. "I think we'd better get you up to the room."

"Okay," he said obligingly. "I'll just stop at the bar and get another drink first."

"Oh, no you don't." Rising, she took his arm and began to steer him her way. "I'm in charge for the rest of the evening," she told him happily. "You're going to do what I tell you to do."

"Okay," he said.

She laughed as she led him to the elevator. If only everything were this easy.

Chapter Eight

The room was swimming, circling, wavering, and James tried hard to concentrate. Damn. He was drunk. He hadn't been like this for years, not since college. What a stupid thing to do. He closed his eyes and lay back on the bed, but the spinning only got worse. He had to reach out and hold on to something so that he wouldn't fall off the world.

"Hey," Kyra said as his arms closed around her. "I'm trying to get you ready for bed here."

"Bed," he murmured, and pulled her down close to him.

"James!"

She was struggling. He frowned.

"Hold still," he muttered. "I feel sick."

She went very quiet very quickly. He sighed, relieved, and snuggled against her. His face was buried in her hair. She smelled like California poppies looked when they covered the hills with gold in the spring. His arm was draped across her, and she felt soft and comforting. He snuggled closer.

"Don't go," he whispered. "Stay with me."

She lay very still, hardly breathing. He was hard and warm and he felt like…like chocolate tasted— rich and smooth and very bad for her. She thought of his kiss, how she melted every time he took her in his arms. He probably thought she was love-starved. And, darn it all, he would be right! It felt so good to lie beside him this way, to hear his breathing, to feel his body heat. But she really had to get away from him. If she didn't watch out, she might come to like this sort of thing a bit too much for comfort.

He was asleep. She drew back, carefully disentangling herself from his arms, and looked down at him. His hair was mussed and his eyes closed, but otherwise, he looked as handsome as ever. She sat and watched him breathe for a few minutes, and a feeling grew inside her, swelling until it almost choked her. She bit her lip and fought it back. What the heck was it, anyway? Appreciation? Affection? Or something stronger?

She couldn't afford to let herself develop anything stronger. She was doing this to get out of debt and protect her grandmother, nothing more. If she ever forgot that, she would be asking for heartbreak. She had to remember that. But it didn't hurt to dream a little, did it?

What would it be like to be really married to, well, to a man like this? For years she'd pushed thoughts of marriage to the back of her mind. If it happened, it happened, but she wasn't going to make it the main goal of her life. She'd been disillusioned when Gary had left her high and dry after her parents' accident. If you couldn't count on a man to be there for you when things went really bad, what good was he, anyway? She harbored a deep resentment for the way she'd been abandoned and she'd been determined never to leave herself that vulnerable again.

Now she'd suddenly had this faux marriage thrust at her and it was bringing to the surface thoughts and longings she'd suppressed for a long, long time. To have her own man, children, a home of her own. Wasn't that the fundamental dream of every woman?

Oh well. Enough of that. She had to get him ready for bed. Leaning over him, she felt hesitant. How was she going to undress him without bringing on some very specific feelings? *Pretend you're a nurse,* she told herself silently. *Or a doctor. They have to hold themselves aloof from what they are doing all the time.*

She reached for his belt, unbuckled it and pulled it out from around him, then reached to unbutton and unzip his slacks. Aloof or not, suddenly her heart was beating as though she were running a mile on a track and her face was hot and red, even though there was no one there to see her. She clamped her lips together and hardened herself. One tug, then another, and his slacks were slipping down. She pulled them off and threw a blanket over him as quickly as she could. She wasn't going to look! Well, maybe just a tiny bit, just before the blanket landed.

And then she hated herself. *I can't believe I did that!*

But that was all she was going to do. She rose and turned out the light, walking to her bedroom without looking back. She was going to go to bed and go right to sleep and not think about anything! There were some things better dealt with in the morning light.

She woke in sunlight and looked at the clock. It was still early, but they had a big day ahead. She'd better get up.

The first thing she wanted to do was call home and see how her grandmother was doing. She got Nurse O'Brien and chatted with her for a few minutes. Everything was fine at home. That reassured her.

Now to face James. She squared her shoulders and marched out into the main room.

He was still asleep. She went to the bed, looked at him and smiled. She couldn't help it. So she had an affection for him. So what? She was allowed to enjoy this whole caper just a little, wasn't she?

Well, maybe. Just as long as she didn't let herself fall in love.

Suddenly, she was ravenous. She pulled out the room service menu and gasped at the prices. There was no way she was spending a full day's salary on a cup of coffee and a Danish! These people were robbers. She threw down the menu and went to the bathroom to wash up and comb her hair. She would go down to the coffee shop herself.

She made the trek to the ground floor and spent some time browsing in the gift shop before heading for the coffee shop and breakfast. The order was still hideously expensive, but about half the price room service would have been. She had everything packed to go and took it back up, balancing the box against the door as she fumbled for her entry card. And then she was in the room.

James was up. Well, sort of up. He was sitting at the table, propped against the back of the chair in a strange way, his eyes barely slits in his handsome face.

"Good morning," she said cheerfully.

"Arrgghh," he answered. The sound seemed to be a cry from the depths of his soul.

"It looks like a lovely day," she chirped as she made space on the table for her box of goodies. "How do you feel?"

He just glared at her, his eyes flashing from behind lowered lids.

She gave him a big smile. "That's what I love about alcohol," she said as she set her own coffee cup on the table. "It's such a clear-cut vice. When you overindulge, you pay for it right away. Cause and effect. Punishment is swift and sure. You know exactly what you did to bring on the misery." She stood back, hands on her hips, and regarded him dispassionately. "It's supposed to teach you never to do it again."

He winced, his hand to his head. "Could you whisper, please?" he asked in a low, hoarse voice.

"What was that?" she asked sweetly, not lowering her voice at all. "Could you speak up, please? I can't hear you."

He closed his eyes and his moan sounded like a whimper. He was so pathetic, she had immediate pangs of remorse.

"Here, have some orange juice," she urged him, taking the cup out of the box.

He shook his head, looking forlorn.

"Coffee?" she coaxed.

He looked at it suspiciously, but he finally nodded.

"Here you go." She set it before him, then sat and watched as he drank very, very carefully. The drink seemed to do its work. A tiny spark of life appeared in his eyes. "Why don't you take a shower?" she suggested, actually beginning to feel sorry for him. "Everything feels better after a shower."

He nodded, wincing, and stood carefully, as though he might break if he moved too quickly. She watched until he was in the bathroom and had closed the door, and then she grabbed a pillow to smother the sound of her laughter. Poor baby, he was so miserable!

Half an hour later, he seemed almost human once more. He sat across from her at the table again, but now he was nibbling on a roll and trying the orange juice as well.

"Okay," he said firmly, fixing her with a stern look that was only slightly tarnished by the fact that his eyes were still bloodshot. "Okay, just let me explain one thing to you," he said, waving a finger at her. "I don't do this. Not ever."

"You don't do what?" she asked innocently.

"Drink too much. Don't start thinking that you've tied yourself to a year of misery with a drunk." He made a face and put the orange juice down. "I mean, I'll have a glass of wine at dinner every now and then, but I don't do much more than that."

"I know," she said quietly. "I've seen you enough to understand that."

"I just...I don't know." He didn't seem to believe

that she was convinced. "I haven't done anything like this since college. I don't know why..."

"I think I know," she said softly, raising her chin. "You're in as much turmoil about what we're going to do today as I am." She smiled at him. "We're both a couple of cowards."

He blinked, then favored her with something that was almost a grin. "Maybe you're right," he said. Then he frowned and ran a hand through his hair. "Why do Elvis Presley songs keep running through my head?" he commented.

She gave him a wide-eyed look. "I haven't a clue," she murmured. Glancing at her watch, she tried to keep from getting nervous. "What time did you say the ceremony is?"

"Four o'clock."

She stretched her arms above her head and gave her back a twist, then rested her hands on her head. "What are we going to do until then?"

"I don't know." His eyes glinted appreciatively. He'd liked that stretch. "Want to go to lunch a little later?"

She hesitated, avoiding his gaze. "Where? Are you planning to see any of your friends again today?"

"My friends?"

Her gaze flickered up to meet his, then dropped again. "Those people from last night."

"No. Why?"

She mumbled something but his eyes were narrowing. "You don't feel comfortable around them, do you?"

"Well...no."

"There's no reason you shouldn't be comfortable with them."

She gave him a baleful look. "Oh please. I could give you a list."

"Okay. Do it. Tell me what bothers you about them."

She let her tongue draw a quick line of moisture on her lower lip as she considered just how honest to be. It wasn't a difficult decision. Why should she hide her feelings at this point? "Okay," she said, looking into his gaze with her own clear-eyed honesty. "Let's see. Maybe it's because they're all rich and famous, and I'm not. Or maybe it's because they're all really well-educated, and I'm not. Or maybe it's the clothes. They dress Fifth Avenue. I dress small-town yard sale. Are you beginning to get the picture?"

He was looking at her as though she'd lost her mind. "This is complete lunacy. Rich and famous people are still just people. They are no different than anyone else." He grimaced. "Hell, you're a better person than ninety percent of them."

She bit back a pleased smile. "Only ninety percent?" she said.

"Well, there are about ten percent that I don't know that well, so I can't say." He frowned thoughtfully, studying her. "Kyra, you're worth ten of any of them. Didn't your mother ever tell you that real worth comes from inside? I wish..." He shook his head. "Well, I can't make you rich and famous or get you a college degree, but there is one thing we can do." He rose, a look of determination on his face. "We can sure as hell get you some clothes."

She gasped. That wasn't what she'd been angling for. "Oh, no. Oh James, I didn't mean for you to…"

He grabbed her hand and pulled her close, his jaw firm again. "Will you just be quiet and let me take care of things? We're going to be married in a few hours. There's no time to lose!"

There shouldn't have been enough hours in the day to do what they did next. James contacted the concierge, Mrs. Denigrew, and told her their problem. When she found out what was at stake and that a wedding was being planned, she took over immediately, demanding details and making lists. Commandeering one of the smaller banquet rooms, she put in calls to the major department stores and a few dress boutiques, and requested emergency service. She took Kyra's measurements and put her in a comfortable chair while the representatives arrived, each with a model of Kyra's size to exhibit the clothing. James came to sit beside her and they watched the young ladies sashay through the room. Kyra was supposed to point out what she liked and what she didn't. At first, she didn't realize that she was setting an outfit aside for herself each time she made a favorable comment.

When she did, she grabbed James by the sleeve. "What are we doing? I can't afford these clothes!"

He gave her a sardonic look. "I can."

"No." She stood, putting her foot down, as it were. "Stop! This isn't right. We can't waste these people's time like this. I'm not going to be able to buy any of these things!"

"Kyra, I told you. I'm buying them."

Her eyes were full of injured pride. "No. You're

paying me a salary. We never said anything in the contract about clothes.''

James gazed at her, bemused. She really seemed to mean it. She must know by now that he was willing to pay for anything she wanted. Most women he knew would be only too glad to take advantage of that. Was she really different? Or was this all an act?

"Every job has its required uniform," he said dryly. "Think of this as a chance to stock up. You need to wear these things in order to be married to me. Right? And since you can't afford to buy them, I'll do it.''

She looked at the models, unsure of what to do. "We'll keep track," she muttered. "I'll pay you back.''

"Relax," he told her. "We'll just pick out a few things. Don't worry about it." He gestured with a toss of his head toward where the models stood poised, unsure whether to leave the room or go on. "Let them do their job, Kyra," he told her softly. "They've come all the way over here.''

She sank back into her seat. He was right, of course. And it was awfully fun to see these beautiful things and to pretend she might wear them. But it worried her, too. She was being paid for this job. She didn't want to get into a position where she was so obligated to James that she didn't feel she could go against him on anything.

Still, it was exciting. These clothes were like nothing she'd ever owned, made of the finest fabrics, put together with care and attention to style and fit. There was no way to keep from wanting them. There was a powder-blue slacks-and-sweater set that she adored, and a few others items she would love to have.

Maybe she could afford to buy one or two of them. With planning, maybe she could get a couple of basic things and build a wardrobe around them. It was a thought, anyway.

James was watching her more than he was scoping out the clothing styles—or even the models, pretty as they were. His head was still pounding, but his thinking was beginning to clear. And he was coming to the conclusion that Kyra Symington was different from any other woman he'd ever known. And at the moment, he wasn't sure if that was good or bad.

He still hadn't made up his mind when Mrs. Denigrew came bustling in, carrying her notebook and pencil at the ready, and asked where the wedding was to take place.

"Uh, The Little Chapel of Love," James told her.

Her middle-aged face didn't give away her emotions often, but on this one, her horror was plain. "Oh no. That won't do at all."

James seemed to be putty in her hands. "It won't?"

"No." She looked as though the very thought might make her faint. "It's a horrible place."

That had been Kyra's opinion as well, but she hadn't wanted to bring it up. She watched their exchange with interest.

"Well," James said doubtfully, "we're booked there at four."

"Don't worry." Mrs. Denigrew patted his hand like a kindly aunt. "I'll get you out of it. We have a small chapel right here in the hotel. It's a lovely room. Fresh flowers every day." She jotted something down in her ever-present notebook. "I'll get a minister for you. And you'll need witnesses."

James looked a little overwhelmed. "Well, maybe..."

"Don't think twice. I'm taking care of everything." Mrs. Denigrew smiled reassuringly and hurried off.

Kyra had to laugh at the expression on James's face. "I'm going to have to study this woman's technique," she told him. "She seems to have your number."

He didn't laugh, but he did grab her hand and hold it, and once he'd done that, she couldn't think about anything else. The clothes were beginning to blur, anyway. Enough was enough. So when he suggested they go to lunch, she was ready.

But she couldn't eat.

They sat in the glass-tower room of a neighboring hotel, watching Las Vegas spin beneath them. Looking out, they could see the purple mountain range on the far horizon, and the golden desert in between. They talked about inconsequential things—the waiter's haircut, the voice of the woman at the next table, the heat, their favorite foods.

And then Kyra noticed that he wasn't eating either.

"Are you nervous?" she teased him.

"Hell, yes," he replied, his gaze skimming over her recklessly. "Hey, I'm getting married, lady. It's going to change everything. I'm supposed to be nervous."

"But it's not real," she reminded him, pretending she wasn't nervous herself—though one look at the way she was twisting her hands together, lacing and unlacing her fingers, would have given anyone a clue. "It's just a business deal. Remember?"

"You know what?" he said softly, leaning closer.

"It's getting more and more difficult to keep that in mind."

Her heart skipped a beat. She knew exactly what he was talking about. It was hard. One moment she was seduced into pretending this was real, that they could possibly be in love, that it was okay to open her heart to him. And the next, she had to bring her guard up, hold back again, and remember that this was temporary and not real at all. Whatever it was, it was going to be over in a year. If she actually let herself do something crazy—like fall in love—she would be in big trouble.

It was hard to remember that, because this getting-married stuff was fun. And so was being with James.

"But you have to remember," she said quickly. "We both do."

"Do we?"

He looked at her and suddenly their surface conversation melted away. His turquoise eyes were smoky, filled with an awareness of her, a sensuality that seemed to reach out and touch her. His gaze dropped to her lips, then made a slow, tantalizing trip down the line of her neck, and she felt as though his fingers were travelling that path, tracing a pattern of sizzling sensation wherever they touched. She could hardly breathe. The moment seemed to stretch into an eternity and she felt a yearning begin to build inside her, a need that burned for attention.

James's cellular phone rang. It took a moment for them to react, and then it was as though they were waking from a dream. He took the call, made a few one-word answers, then clicked it off and looked at her casually, his intensity of a moment before seemingly forgotten.

"That was Mrs. Denigrew," he said dryly. "She says to get back. Your hair appointment is in ten minutes."

"My hair appointment? What hair appointment?"

He shrugged. "She's obviously made you one." He frowned. "We may have to escape from this woman under cover of darkness."

Kyra smiled. "She's wonderful. I should have made a hair appointment myself, but I thought…" She let her words fade away without telling him that she'd thought it too extravagant a thing to do for a phony ceremony. But the wedding was beginning to take on more importance, and she wasn't sure why.

She glanced at her watch. She was getting married in two hours. Suddenly her mouth was very dry.

Chapter Nine

Music swelled behind Kyra, an organ playing the wedding march. It was on compact disc, but that didn't matter. The sound was huge and thrilling. She was wearing a wedding gown Mrs. Denigrew had found for her. It had a fitted bodice covered with lace and seed pearls, with pagoda sleeves and a draped neckline. The resourceful woman had also come up with a bouquet of tiny, trailing white flowers that Kyra carried before her. She hesitated for another moment, looking down at the end of the aisle. James was waiting for her, his face lighted up as though this were for real. She swept toward him as though she thought the same thing. Suddenly she realized something: she'd never been so happy.

The chapel was small, with five pews on each side, which were half filled with people Mrs. Denigrew had corralled to come as witnesses to this marriage. It looked as though she'd pulled in everyone she could find who admitted to knowing anyone named

James. Still, the man knew an amazing amount of people—at least among the wealthy who stayed here at the Camelot. Kyra marvelled as she walked steadily down the aisle. You could almost make believe this was the real thing. And she couldn't help herself—she loved it.

Things hadn't been so sanguine an hour earlier, when Mrs. Denigrew had absolutely nixed her white suit and pulled out the wedding gown for her to use instead. Kyra had been appalled. She couldn't afford a gown like that.

"Never mind," Mrs. Denigrew said. "You're not buying anything here. It's merely rented for two hours."

Kyra hadn't been mollified. She'd thought it was somehow sacrilegious to wear the gown in pretense. But Mrs. Denigrew had worn her down. And once she'd put it on, she'd been caught up in the moment. She did look awfully good in it. That, along with the way her hair was piled atop her head with only adorable tendrils hanging down around her face and the pearl tiara snugly in place made her look like a princess. She could see from the expression on James's face that the whole thing had worked. He was awestruck.

Awestruck and devastatingly handsome in his black tails and tie. He took a step forward to meet her. She put her hand in his and he led her into position in front of the minister.

"My God," he whispered before he let her go. "You're stunning."

She glowed with his praise. She felt stunning. She felt as though she were a different person, and more, that things would never be the same again. The minister was saying words that rang like declarations in her heart. This might be pretend, but she was caught up in it as though it were real, and she felt herself glowing with the elation of it.

"I do," she said when the time came.

He slipped a ring onto her hand, and she put a ring on his finger. The minister pronounced them husband and wife. James leaned forward to kiss her. She kissed him back with so much emotion, she was afraid for a moment that tears would come.

But the recessional boomed out just in time, and they turned and smiled at the congregation. Everyone leaped to their feet and began to clap. Mrs. Denigrew opened the double doors to the next room where she'd set up champagne and little silver cookies on golden trays.

And a wedding cake! With a miniature bride and groom on top. Kyra and James, still holding hands, looked at each other and laughed. It was all so perfect, it was almost funny.

They spent the next hour enjoying their reception. People milled around each of them and they were pulled farther and farther apart, until James had his contingent on one side of the room and she had hers on the other. She would look across the heads and smile at him, and he would look across the heads and wink at her. But they were so far apart.

She had never been the center of attention like this before, and to her surprise, she really liked it. What was more, now that she was in a designer dress and had her hair piled stylishly, now that she was officially part of James's life, the attitude toward her was very different. People who had sneered at her the night before were deferring to her, making a point to come to speak to her, waiting in line to get her attention. She was the princess. Their smiles were wide and seemingly genuine. They liked her now. She was still the same person, only in different packaging. It wasn't right. It wasn't fair. But it was reality and she might as well face it. Just as long as she didn't give in to it and didn't believe in it, she told herself. Because it could disappear as suddenly as it had come. *Real worth comes from inside.* Who had said that to her? James. She turned to catch his eye but he was busy talking to a gray-haired gentleman who was clapping him on the back as though they were old friends. And they probably were.

She had a momentary qualm, realizing that these were *all* James's friends. Not one was hers. Suddenly she missed her grandmother badly. And the girls from the office. And even Mollie, her friend who was always trying to set her up with her terrible brother-in-law. If only she had somebody, anybody, of her own here.

James turned to look at her, and suddenly his face changed. He gaped and she turned to see what he was looking at. To her surprise, an old friend she'd just made the night before was coming to her rescue.

"Elvis!" she cried, opening her arms to him.

"Hello, sugar," he said, his mouth twisted in the patented sneer of a grin. His bell-bottomed suit was mint-green this day, with little gold sequins up and down the seams, and the sunglasses he wore had emerald panes. He carried his guitar in one hand and a silk handkerchief in the other, and he was a welcome sight for Kyra. "May I give the bride a kiss for luck?" he asked.

"Of course you can." She offered her cheek and

he gave her a nice one, and a quick hug to go with it.

"I don't think you oughta worry about things, honey," he told her as he drew back. "I saw you and your boy James together, and I think it's the real thing. It feels so right."

Her smile was noncommittal. "Thank you," she told him sincerely. "You've been a big help." And she reached up and gave him a kiss on his cheek, for which he looked bashful as he backed away to the laughter and applause of the knot of people around them.

James reached her side as Elvis was melting into the crowd.

"Hey," he said, looking after the retreating green figure and then down at her with a frown. "What was *he* doing here?"

She smiled at him and flipped back a curling tendril of hair that had been hanging over her face. "You have your friends. I have mine."

They cut the cake. Kyra threw her bouquet. The small crowd was finally thinning. They waved good-bye to the last of them, and then they retreated to Mrs. Denigrew's office before making their way upstairs.

"Here you are," that efficient lady said, handing them a plastic bag full of things. "The guestbook, filled out by your guests. Some wedding presents people left for you. And, uh, oh yes, a videotape of your wedding. The entire ceremony and the arrival of some of your guests."

"A videotape?" Kyra looked at her, dumbfounded. "How did you do all this at such short notice?"

Mrs. Denigrew's perfect lips formed a practiced smile. "My dear, I can do anything. Think of me as your fairy godmother."

And that was what it seemed like as Kyra slipped into a private dressing room to remove her wedding gown and return to her new powder-blue slacks-and-sweater outfit. She wouldn't have been too surprised if she'd found a pumpkin and a few scattered mice when she went back inside Mrs. Denigrew's office. Kyra knew her night of enchantment was over. She sighed and smiled at James. It was time to go back to their room.

They were still riding on a cloud as they let themselves into the room. They kicked off their shoes and James loosened his tie and they flopped onto couches and went over the happenings of the past couple of hours, laughing about incidents they'd shared. He asked her about Elvis and she kept him guessing. She asked him about some of the women who had seemed a little too friendly with him, and he teased her about them. Then he told her that some of his friends had an outing planned for the next day. They were to be the guests of honor. Harry Babcock, a wealthy rancher who raised racehorses, had promised to sell him a horse he'd had his eye on at a very good price—"Consider it a wedding present," he'd said. James was excited. He'd been looking for a good racehorse for a long time. Kyra shook her head. She'd married a man who wanted to have a racehorse. This was completely insane.

A knock on the door brought a lobster supper from room service. Kyra chided James on the cost of all they had done that day, and he told her it was not a day for counting pennies. They were both as hungry as wolves. They ate every speck of food the waiter had brought them.

They sat on one couch when they were finished, talking softly. James took out his cuff links and rolled up his sleeves, revealing his strong, muscular forearms covered lightly with dark hair. Kyra found her gaze straying there as she told him about her childhood, about how she had spent a lot of time at her grandmother's house because her parents were often gone on trips together, how her grandmother had raised her almost as much as her mother had. And James unbuttoned his shirt halfway down, showing off a tanned chest that gleamed in the lamplight as he told her about going on digs with his aunt, how close they had been, how she so often got her way with him.

"Do you know she threatened to buy a mail-order bride for me if I didn't get married in the next year?" he told her.

Her mouth dropped. She wasn't sure if she was looking forward to meeting this aunt or not. "You're kidding."

"Would I kid about a thing like that? She was getting catalogs. 'Better a catalog than a singles bar,' she told me. I was afraid I was going to come home some night and find an immigrant with a knapsack over her shoulder waiting on my doorstep."

Kyra frowned at him. "But I thought she was trying to get you to marry someone named Jalopy."

"That came later. When I was absolutely adamant about no catalogs. She got on the Jalopy Clark bandwagon and I could see there was no getting out of this one. Unless..." He let that thought trail off as though it was suddenly an awkward thing to talk about.

"Unless you hired someone to marry you," she stated flatly.

He nodded and didn't meet her gaze. In the meantime, he unbuttoned the rest of the buttons on his shirt and left it hanging open. Kyra knew it was time to leave the room and get into her own space, away from his provocative presence, but somehow she couldn't make herself leave just yet. They sat together silently for a few minutes, and then his head came up. "Hey, I forgot. We have to call her."

"Who?"

"Aunt Jo." He reached for the telephone. "We have to tell her what we've done."

Kyra watched him dial. "What time is it in Egypt?" she asked.

"It doesn't matter," he told her with a wicked light in his eyes. "I like waking her up. It throws her off guard and she can't fight back as well." His face changed. "Aunt Jo! Here I am again. Just thought you ought to know—we did it. We're married."

"Oh, James." She sighed. "Why can't you call me at a decent hour?"

"Because I know you like to keep up on the news, and this is breaking right now. I've married Kyra Symington Redman. I'll be faxing you a copy of the marriage certificate in the morning."

"James, are you serious?"

"Yes, my dear aunt, I am very serious. So you might as well call off the visit from the Clarks. There's no point to it now."

"James, my dear James. Number one, I'm writing you out of my will. Number two, I'm flying home as soon as I can get a flight. I have to see this for myself. Number three, I can't stop the Clarks. They're on a tramp steamer somewhere in the middle of the Pacific. They will arrive next week, as scheduled. And number four, we'll all have to stay in your apartment, because my house is being painted inside and out. See you soon darling. Kiss the bride for me." And she was gone.

James stared at the receiver, swearing softly. Kyra hadn't heard what Aunt Jo had said, but she could see that James felt he'd been bested again. She started to say something teasing, then thought better of it. Something about the look on his face told her this was no time for levity.

"Well," she said, starting to gather herself toward making the trek to her room.

His attention was back on her and he slid closer. "Where do you think you're going?" he asked, reaching for her.

"I..." She didn't get any further. His arms closed around her, pulling her close, and he began to trail a line of kisses up her neck. "James," she protested weakly, shivering.

"Hmm?" he replied, taking her earlobe between his teeth. "You said something?"

His tongue slid along the edge of her ear and she gasped at the sweet sensation. His breath was warm and tickling against her skin, and his lips touched so smoothly.... His mouth was on hers as soon as she turned her face his way, tasting her as though she were some rare wine to be carefully drunk, drinking from her as though this was just the beginning, just the start of a long, long night of lovemaking he'd been planning for a long, long time. His hands, his mouth, his body, all seemed to be caressing her. It was pure ecstasy. She'd never felt anything so delicious in her life. She knew she had to make a stand and make it fast, or she wasn't going to be able to do it.

"James," she said breathlessly, tearing away from his kiss. "No, we can't…"

"Can't we?" he asked softly, his eyes smoldering. He reached to pull her back into his arms. "Why not?"

She put up her hands to fend him off, but when her palms came in contact with the hot, smooth skin of his chest, heat seemed to pour into her body and spread like a fire in her veins. He felt so good. Her hands slipped down, caressing his rounded muscles. She'd never felt anything so alive, so exciting…so sexy. His head went back and his body moved to her touch and he groaned with pleasure. She gasped at the power she had, a power she'd never known—a power so strong, it frightened her, and she tried to draw back. He reached out and circled her wrists with his hands, forcing her hands back onto his body. At the same time, he leaned forward to kiss her again, and she leaned toward him, too, wanting to have his tongue.

And then she wanted more, so much more, and so wildly, that she cried out with the need for him, a need that was kindled deep inside her body. A small cry, but a cry nonetheless, and that startled her into an awareness of just what was happening.

"No." She pulled away with sudden force that caught him off guard. "No, James. We can't." She said it fiercely this time, moving away from him on the couch as she did so.

He was blinking at her as though she'd just turned on the light in a darkened room. "Why?" he said.

"Because we're not really married," she told him as firmly as she could, hoping her voice wouldn't shake. "We're only married on paper. We're not...we're not married in our hearts."

He reared back as though she'd slapped him. She rose unsteadily and forced herself to hurry across the carpet. "I have to get ready for bed," she told him.

He watched her go and didn't say a word. She closed herself in her room and leaned on the door, catching her breath. That was the hardest thing she'd ever done in her life.

Chapter Ten

Kyra heard the phone ring as if through a foggy haze. She'd hardly slept all night, and when she'd finally drifted into real sleep, there went the telephone. She heard James answering it, so she waited, trying to drive away the lingering grogginess.

But when James appeared in her doorway, she came fully awake very quickly.

"It's your Nurse O'Brien," he told her. "Your grandmother has taken a turn for the worse."

"What?" She sat up in bed, pulling the covers to her chest. "What's happened?"

"She said not to worry. The doctor thinks it's not too serious. But she has been coughing and they want her in the hospital so that they can guard against pneumonia."

She stared at him for a long moment, then slipped out of bed, heedless that he was going to see her in her skimpy white lace baby-doll pajamas. "I'll have to get back right away," she said, feeling defensive.

If he was going to raise any objections, she was ready to fight. She knew he'd been planning a few days of honeymoon, but this was more important. Men never seemed to understand how things had to work with families. She certainly didn't expect him to want to do anything to help, but that didn't matter. This was her grandmother and it was up to her.

"Of course," he said, his gaze skimming lightly over her breasts, visible beneath the flimsy fabric. "I'll call the airline and get us on the next flight out."

She turned and looked at him, wide-eyed. "Oh, you don't have to go," she said, her surprise showing on her face. "I can go alone." Then she smiled weakly, trying to lighten the mood. "Don't you have to see a man about a horse?"

He shrugged, not making a move toward her as he might have on any other occasion in the past two days if he'd seen her so provocatively clad. "I can see that man some other time. I'm going with you."

She searched his eyes. "You told me this was special. That he was going to give you an exceptional price as a wedding gift."

"It doesn't matter, Kyra. What matters is you and your grandmother."

She stared at him. She still didn't believe it. She frowned. "James, really, you don't have to. I can handle this on my own."

He threw her a look that she would have called disgusted if she'd been paying enough attention to see it. He went into the main room and called the airline while she began to wash up and dress.

So he was coming with her. She appreciated that but she assumed he must have some reason of his

own for wanting to do it. She couldn't think why
else he would come. She was used to handling things
on her own. Still, she had to admit it felt good to
have a shoulder to lean on, even if she didn't really
do much leaning. She'd been standing on her own
for so long, she was afraid she didn't know how to
accept help very graciously.

A few hours later they were in James's car, heading up the coast from the Los Angeles airport. Kyra
was worried and anxious to get to her grandmother's
side, but despite her preoccupation, she'd noticed
that James was unusually withdrawn and quiet. And
he hadn't tried to touch her once all day. She imagined he was still angry about the night before. She
winced, thinking about it, wishing it could have been
some other way. She knew he'd felt rejected, but she
hadn't expected it to affect him quite so thoroughly.

Well, if that was the case, he was just going to
have to be angry. Because she wasn't going to make
love with him. They had decided that from the first,
hadn't they? They both knew it would be a disaster
to get that close. She couldn't risk it. She just wasn't
going to let herself be that stupid. If she was honest
with herself, she would have to admit that she was
too darn close to falling in love with him as it was.
She had to be on her guard.

Falling in love. What a concept. How could you
love a man you barely knew, even if you were married to him? And yet, every time she looked at him,
she felt something warm and wonderful surge
through her veins. She cared about him. She wanted
to make him smile. She wanted to see him happy.
Was that a part of love? She had to think it was. And
yet, it didn't guarantee anything at all. Maybe it was

infatuation. Who knew? At any rate, she wasn't going to risk making it worse. She knew what happened to women who assumed too much. And it wasn't going to happen to her. Not again.

They got to the hospital a little after noon. Kyra's heart stopped for a moment when she saw her grandmother. She looked so small and frail with the tubes and wires attached to her, all bringing her liquid medication or running monitors that flashed and beeped. She was drifting in and out of sleep, but she woke long enough to kiss Kyra and to faintly congratulate her new husband, beaming at him.

She clutched Kyra's hand and whispered, "I'm so glad you're married. Now you won't look so sad any more."

Kyra had to turn away to hide her tears. Her gaze met James's and held for a moment, but she couldn't read the emotion in his eyes.

Her grandmother went back to sleep and Kyra sat with her for a while, but James seemed to spend most of his time talking to doctors, so she was hardly surprised that he had a new angle on things when they left to go to his apartment.

"The doctors say she can't come home for quite some time, but once the threat of pneumonia passes, she won't need hospital care. They recommend a nursing home called Avignon, which has a complete medical staff and equipment for emergencies on hand. I think we should go check it out this afternoon."

She looked at him in surprise. "It's a wonderful place," she acknowledged. "I've done quite a bit of research on this myself, since the threat has loomed that we might have to do something like that. But, James, it's so expensive.''

"Let's talk about that later, after we've been out to see the place,'' he said brusquely, cutting her off. "Right now, I just want to get back to my apartment and have some lunch.''

She swallowed her protestations. He was still upset with her, that much was obvious. Having him come on to her all the time was agony, but she had a feeling this coldness could get to be ten times worse. She snuck a look at him as they rode through town. His profile was solid as granite, and just as unforgiving.

His penthouse apartment was something else again. She was intimidated at first. It looked like a showcase. Did anyone human actually live here?

Standing in the middle of the living room, she turned slowly, taking it all in. "Did you do the decorating yourself?'' she asked dryly.

James glanced around the room as though he'd never noticed it before. Chrome and glass and a white carpet. A modern sculpture. A painting that looked as though someone had created it by gluing together old rags—but the colors matched the upholstery. He'd brought in an interior decorator when he'd first moved in, given him free rein, and hadn't given it a thought since. But it looked just fine to him. All he'd ever done there was sleep, anyway. What else had he needed?

Was it going to be different now? Was it going to be a home just because Kyra was there with him? That was a question that intrigued him, but one he didn't want to deal with at the moment.

"No," he said in answer to her question. "I hired someone."

"That's a relief," she said with a quick smile.

He hesitated. "If there's anything you want to change, go ahead," he told her. "Make the place more comfortable if you want to."

She flushed. Everything was always complicated by the strange status of their relationship. She looked at the wallpaper and shook her head. "I don't think I should do that, James. After all, I'm just here temporarily. I'm just an employee...."

His face darkened. He uttered a four-letter word and stalked out of the room, leaving her to stare after him in bewilderment. After all, this was his setup. He'd hired her. What did the man want from her?

They had some lunch and he drove her over to her house so that she could pick up some clothes and her own car. Later, they went together to see the nursing home. It was a lovely place overlooking the ocean, with courtyards and friendly nurses. Everything looked very clean and well equipped. Kyra considered it all with longing, then was a little short with James. She was just a bit resentful that he'd made her come to see this. It was way out of reach for her and her grandmother. There was no way they could ever afford it. Why bother to raise expectations this way? She was going to have to take a look at more reasonable places.

They didn't talk much on the way back to the hospital. Her grandmother looked a little better. Kyra sat with her for half an hour, then kissed her good-night and came out of the room in time to hear James making arrangements with the doctor on the telephone near the nurses' station. Arrangements that seemed to involve her grandmother.

"What are you doing?" she asked as he got off the phone.

"Finalizing some plans." His turquoise gaze swept over her dispassionately, and then he took her arm and began to walk her toward the exit and the parking lot. "I was hoping we would be able to bring your grandmother to live with us when she was released," he told her. "But the doctor thinks she needs to be under more intensive care than anything we could do at home, at least for the next few weeks. So I'm having her moved to Avignon as soon as—"

"James!" She whirled to face him, stopping him in his tracks. "You have no right to make plans for my grandmother. She's *my* grandmother. I'll make her plans."

He actually looked surprised at her anger. "I thought we'd agreed Avignon would be best for her. It's a beautiful place."

She turned and began to walk again, as much to deal with her fury as to get to the car. "She is not going to Avignon," she announced firmly.

He kept up with her pace. "But it is by far the best—"

"Of course it's the best," she snapped, giving him a scathing look. "It's also the most expensive. We can't afford it."

His face was set. "Yes, we can."

They were leaving the building and had to wait while a group of nurses entered. Once they were outside, she turned on him again.

"Yes *you* can," she said, eyes flashing. "My grandmother and I can't."

"Kyra, I'm paying for it."

Didn't he understand anything? "No you're not. I can't let you do that."

"What do you mean, let me do it? We're married. Remember? This is what married people do. They take care of each other and they take care of their families. We're all part of the same family now, whether you like it or not."

Suddenly she felt very tired. "No, James, you know that's not true. This isn't a real marriage. And I can't afford a place like that."

He looked about ready to tear his hair out. "You don't have to afford it. Aren't you listening?"

She held her shoulders stiffly. "I can't let you do it."

"That's too bad," he said harshly. "Because I'm not doing it for you. I'm doing it for your grandmother."

She bit her lip, staring at the horizon, and he let out a long, exasperated breath. "Kyra, I want to do it."

She turned to look at him and suddenly he took her hands in his, gazing deeply into her eyes, searching for something, a connection, a sign. "Kyra," he said softly. "Why can't you let me close? Why can't you let me in?"

She was shivering. A sense of panic fluttered in her chest. "I don't know what you're talking about."

He took her chin in his hand and studied her face. "Take some time. Think about it. You might be able to figure it out on your own." He dropped his hand, his mouth twisted into a bittersweet smile. "Since being on your own is what you seem to like best," he said as he turned away.

He got into the car and she followed suit, feeling numb. She didn't completely understand what he'd said or why he'd said it. She only knew that she didn't want to become so obligated to him that she could never be her own person again. That was just too frightening a prospect. Once she'd given over her trust, would he leave her flat? Why not? It was such a pattern. She saw it all around her. She didn't dare risk it.

He drove back slowly. They ate some chicken he picked up at a drive-through on the way home. And then they went to bed in separate rooms.

But every word he'd said kept repeating in Kyra's head. It would be so tempting to believe he really meant it, that he was trying to get close for more than a warm body in his bed. But she was so afraid to depend on him. She'd spent the past few years being strong. If she gave that up, what would she have to fall back on when he disappointed her?

James went back to work the next morning. Kyra decided she'd better take some time off to be with her grandmother.

"I'll tell them you're taking the week off," he told her.

"A whole week?"

"Why not? You'd better get this business with your grandmother settled. Then you can come back with a clear mind to start on the Black Stone Beach project."

At first, she was tempted to resent him for taking charge this way. But the more she thought about it, the more she realized he was being thoughtful, and she was being somewhat ungrateful about it. He really was turning out to be an awfully nice man. And she hadn't been all that nice to him. She regretted that and she vowed to mend her ways. There were things she could do short of becoming a complete dependent. She would have to think about it.

She went in to the hospital. Her grandmother was looking alert and was actually eating some breakfast. Nurse O'Brien came in to visit while Kyra was still there, and her grandmother began to tell her about her pending move to Avignon. Kyra started to correct her, then stopped herself. Maybe it was time she admitted defeat. The doctor must have told her grandmother about James's plans. And since it seemed to make her happy—who was Kyra to rain on this parade? If James was really willing to foot the bill.... She felt so tired, worn out from wrestling with these things.

She told him of her decision that evening at dinner. She'd made scallops and linguine in a light wine sauce and James had to have told her twenty times how good it was. That brightened the atmosphere, and when she told him she'd given in on the nursing home, things got even happier.

But still, he didn't touch her. And whenever she got too close, the wariness was back in his eyes. She began to realize this wasn't just her problem. He seemed to be as hesitant to reach out across the divide between them as she was. They were friendly enough with each other, but some of that spontaneous joy they'd had the day they were married had been lost. Kyra mourned it in her own way, and wished she knew what she could do to bring it back for good.

"You know, I was thinking," he said later that

evening. "They always say that people who are ill
are most comfortable when they can go home and be
in their own bed. If things don't work out for your
grandmother at Avignon—if she doesn't like it
there—we can look into fixing up her bedroom in
her own house. It's not that far from the hospital in
case she needs medical care." He looked at her seriously. "And we might consider moving in with
her."

She stared at him, shocked. "You would be willing to give up living here? Wouldn't that place be
too small for you?"

He shrugged. "All I need is a bed to sleep in."
He frowned at her. "You don't think I need all this,
do you?" he said, gesturing toward the wall hangings
and expensive furniture. "I could be perfectly happy
in a tent." He grinned at her suddenly. "As long as
you were with me," he added.

She laughed. He was kidding with that last comment, she was sure, but she had to admit, he was
always ready to do things for others in a way she
would never have expected from him if she hadn't
known him so well. He was such a good guy. How
was a person supposed to keep from falling for a man
like this?

"Oh, by the way," he told her just before they
went their separate ways to bed, "your friend Chareen came by my office today. She and the others
want to give you a wedding shower next week. I told
her they could have it here. Is that all right with
you?"

"Oh." She was touched that they were thinking
of her. Still…she looked at James's face and decided
not to say what she'd been thinking…that this wasn't

a real marriage and therefore she didn't deserve a real shower. "How nice," she said instead. "That'll be a lot of fun."

He gave her a crooked smile, as though he knew exactly what she'd been thinking and appreciated that she'd avoided saying it. And she realized it hadn't been so hard to suppress it after all.

"Good night," he said, and gave her a quick peck on the cheek.

She closed her eyes when she got into her room and remembered steamier kisses. She never would have guessed that she could miss them—heck, long for them—so very much. But all she had now for comfort in her bed were dreams.

Two days later, Aunt Jo arrived.

She came twenty-four hours before they had expected her and threw them into mass confusion. After all, Aunt Jo was a force to be reckoned with.

She arrived in the evening while they were just finishing dinner. She came in carrying an overnight bag and a huge purse made of Peruvian wool. She gave James a kiss and turned to look at Kyra.

"Hello, my dear," she said, giving her the once-over before giving her a hug. "Welcome to the family."

Kyra murmured something polite and invited her to sit in the living room. The three sat on the edges of chairs and Aunt Jo told them about her trip to Egypt.

While she talked, Kyra studied her with great interest. She couldn't see much of James in her. She had a no-nonsense face and a style of clothing that could only be called bohemian, and those two things

somehow should have clashed, but didn't. Her gray-
ing hair was pulled back into a single braid that hung
down her back. Her dark eyes darted here and there
with a lively curiosity that never seemed satisfied.
And when she smiled, Kyra felt enveloped in
warmth. She was wary at first, but very quickly knew
she was going to like this woman.

They sat talking pleasantly and Aunt Jo reminisced
about James as a child, telling amusing stories about
him that had Kyra laughing. When she got up to go
to the kitchen to get them all something to drink,
James followed her, ostensibly to help carry glasses,
but really to whisper to Kyra, "Quick. Get your stuff
out of your bedroom and put it in mine."

She looked at him in surprise, then realized what
he was saying. He didn't want Aunt Jo to know they
had separate bedrooms. That was sure to arouse her
suspicions. There were five bedrooms in the apartment and she had prepared the one James had told
her his aunt had used once before when she'd stayed
there. But if all Kyra's things were in the room across
the hall, she was sure to notice.

"Oh. Oh, of course." She glanced out at the
woman picking her favorite nuts from the mixed nut
selection in the silver bowl on the coffee table. "You
keep her busy. It'll take a while."

She handed Jo a glass of iced tea and excused
herself, saying she had something she had to take
care of. Then she slipped into the bedroom and
cleared away everything that was out, carrying the
items in a plastic bag and depositing the bag in
James's room. She wasn't going to go as far as emp-
tying drawers and the closet. After all, it made sense
that she might keep some of her things in another

room. She just didn't want to leave it looking as though she slept there.

Which brought up a problem she had thought about fleetingly but hadn't wanted to deal with before. She looked at the large king-size bed that James used. Were she and he going to sleep in his bedroom together? It certainly looked that way. She was going to have to think of something to do about that.

She hurried back and rejoined the talk. Aunt Jo was remembering when James was eighteen and wanted to sign up with the Green Berets.

"I tried to talk him into becoming an Eagle Scout instead, but somehow that didn't have the same panache. It wasn't until I offered to take him with me on a dig in New Guinea that he gave up his military dream."

"It was all a ploy to get her to take me with her from the first," he told Kyra. "She was originally trying to get me to stay behind and go to summer school. That was why I threatened her with the Green Beret stuff."

"A ploy, was it?" Aunt Jo retorted. "Then what was the motivation behind your plans to elope with that little redheaded swimsuit model in your first year at college?"

"Aunt Jo," James said, rolling his eyes. "Please. Not in front of my new bride."

"Oh." She looked at Kyra apologetically. "Sorry. I am having a very hard time remembering that this dear boy is finally married."

"No problem," Kyra responded, with a smile. "I had a feeling he might have had a date or two before we met."

That had both Aunt Jo and James laughing uproariously and Kyra watched their amusement with mixed feelings.

"Well, what do you think of my aunt?" James asked her when they were finally alone in his room.

"She's great," Kyra said, and meant it.

James looked pleased with her answer. "Yeah, she really is. I'm glad she came home to meet you."

"So am I," Kyra said, though she wondered if the reverse was true.

"Wait'll you see her house," he went on. "It's full of mummies and terra-cotta death masks, Carthaginian jewelry and lots of other artifacts. You'll like it."

"I'll bet," she said. But something else was taking up more of her interest right now. They were both in his bedroom. What were they going to do about it? She glanced around the room, then at James. "Well, here we are," she said.

He crossed his arms and looked down at her, amusement glinting in his turquoise eyes. "Yup."

"One bed. Two people." She just wanted to make sure he got that there was a problem here.

"Hey. You can count."

Okay, so he wasn't going to be helpful. "Oh well," she said with a shrug. "I'm sure you won't mind sleeping on the floor."

A slow grin was beginning to creep across his face. "Not a chance," he told her serenely.

"In the bathtub?" she offered hopefully.

"Please."

"Well, then, I will," she announced, heading for the bathroom with her chin in the air.

He grinned, watching her go, and then the grin vanished from his face as he remembered something.

"No! Wait. Don't go in there," he ordered, charging after her.

But it was too late. She was already in, and standing before the calendar, staring at the pretty girl in— and out of—the white fur coat. He reached up to snatch it off the wall, but she beat him to the punch and grabbed it herself.

"Give me that!" he ordered, holding his hand out.

Her chin came up again and her eyes flashed. "Make me," she challenged, spinning and dashing out of the bathroom, calendar in her hand.

He was bigger, faster and stronger, and the next thing she knew, he'd thrown her on the bed and come down on top of her, wrestling her for the calendar. She twisted and turned beneath him, laughing and holding onto the calendar for all she was worth.

"Kyra," he demanded, laughing too, but more serious in his intent. "Come on. Give it to me."

"No!"

"You don't want to look at that thing."

She gave him a mock glare. "Sure I do. I want to see if I can guess which girl you like best."

He went still above her, his hands pinning her shoulders, his gaze on her face. "I thought you already knew," he said softly.

Her heart skipped a beat and she closed her eyes. Why did he say things like that when she knew he couldn't mean it? If only...

His lips touched hers and she opened her eyes again. She wasn't going to let this happen. She'd allowed too much before. She had to keep her wits about her. She...

All rational thought stopped then, because his kiss was warm and sweet and she didn't need to think.

All she needed to do was kiss him back, and she did that, dropping the calendar and lifting her arms to circle his neck and hold him close to her. The weight of his body took on new significance. Her breasts seem to swell beneath the pressure of his chest. A fire sparked deep inside her. If she didn't do something soon, she knew the inevitable would happen, and she would get to the point where she didn't care anymore.

"James. Please stop," she said, twisting her face away from his kiss. "Please."

He hesitated, then rolled off her. "I wish I'd married an ugly troll of a woman," he muttered, his gruff frown making him look like a little boy who'd been denied a cookie. "It would be easier on the instinctive male responses to stimuli."

"So you admit that is all this is?" she challenged.

He lay back and laughed. "I give up," he said. "Don't worry. I'll go."

"Go? What do you mean?"

"There are other bedrooms. Once we're sure she's asleep, I'll sneak down to the far bedroom and sleep there. I'll set an alarm and get back here before she wakes up." He smiled at her, resigned. "Don't worry. She is not an early riser. And if she does catch me down there, I'll just say we had a little spat and I had to vacate your bed for the night. Okay?"

She bit her lip and frowned, feeling like a meanie. He was so willing to do things to make her feel more comfortable. How often did she do things like that for him?

"Don't worry," he said again, touching her cheek with his forefinger. "I'm getting used to this feeling of frustrated lust. I might learn to enjoy it, and then I can become a real martyr.''

She swallowed hard and looked around for something else to talk about. The calendar, the issue that had started all this, was lying, ignored, on the floor. She leaned down to pick it up.

"I'm really sorry to interfere with your recreational reading," she told him, flipping through the pages.

"You don't *read* a calendar." He flushed slightly, definitely looking embarrassed. "Anyway, I'm going to throw it away. Here. I'll rip it up right now."

She rolled away from him, protecting the calendar from his destructive intentions. "Oh no, no, no. I think I can gain a lot of insight into your character and personality from this." She flipped up a page and gazed at a beautiful Asian woman stretched out on a fake tiger-skin rug. "So tell me," she teased. "Which month is your favorite?"

He groaned and grabbed a pillow. "I'm out of here," he grumbled. "You can play around with pictures of half-naked women if you want." He struck a dramatic pose, holding his bedding to his chest. "*I* am making a sacrifice and going to another bedroom. See you in the morning."

He went to the door, opened it slowly, peeking out into the hallway. In another moment, he was gone.

And it was as though an empty place had opened in her heart. She missed him. She threw the calendar onto his dresser, sat cross-legged on the bed and sighed deeply. He was so much fun when he was in a playful mood. And she was just beginning to fully

appreciate how deeply and fundamentally generous
he was.

"Face it, Kyra," she told herself mournfully,
"you little idiot. You're in love."

Chapter Eleven

Kyra had just returned from visiting her grandmother in the hospital when the doorbell rang. She stopped what she was doing, frowning, wondering who this could be. There had been a rash of solicitors in the neighborhood lately, but she'd been sharpening her refusal techniques. She just hated the guilty feelings that cropped up when turning down someone who might or might not be a real charity case.

But her misgivings were misplaced this time. She opened the door and there on the threshold stood a tall, beautiful woman with a fabulous head of auburn hair, dressed in stylish denim with a beige scarf tied casually at her neck.

"Hi," she said, her dark eyes sparkling with friendly amusement. "Is this where James Redman lives?"

"Yes it is." Kyra couldn't help but smile back at the woman. "He's not home at the moment. Can I help you with something?"

"That depends." She glanced down and noticed the rings on Kyra's finger. Her eyes widened. "Tell me that you're married to James," she said, looking pleased as punch. "Make my day."

Kyra laughed. "As a matter of fact, I am married to James. We were married a week ago."

The woman laughed with delight. "I'm saved! Alleluia!" Before Kyra could stop her, she'd reached out and given her a quick hug. "My name is Jill Clark. I've just arrived from Australia. I—"

"No!" Kyra's mouth dropped open. "No, you can't be." She looked up and down at the stunning woman standing before her, incredulous.

"You'd heard I was coming?"

"Oh yes." Suddenly Kyra was laughing along with the woman and ushering her into the room. "Oh, we've been expecting you. Or, I should say, someone with your name." She made a sweeping gesture toward Jill. "But hardly *you*."

"Well, here I am. And I can hardly wait to see James again." She sank onto the couch as though she'd just returned from a long trip—which was pretty much the case. "He was the bane of my existence as a child. Perhaps he's told you? We were sworn enemies most of the time. I think it must have been because we were forced to live together as family for all those years, so we naturally acted like a brother and sister sometimes do. Like rivals."

"Yes, he's told me all about it. But I expected..." She let the sentence dangle. How could she describe to this beautiful, vivacious woman what she'd expected? Instead, she asked about something else. "Where's your mother? I thought she was coming with you."

"Actually, I'm a day ahead of her. She stayed on in San Diego to visit with some friends. She'll be along tomorrow." She shook back her beautiful hair. "To tell you the truth, I thought I'd better come along ahead to warn James of something. But now that he's married, I guess I was worried about nothing."

Kyra propped herself on the arm of a chair. "Did this have anything to do with Aunt Jo and your mother...?"

"Yes! Those two rascals had a plot to try to get James to marry me."

Kyra nodded. "Believe me, he knows about it."

"Does he? So it was being schemed on this end, too. I wasn't sure and I thought I should give him a heads up in case he might blindly fall into one of their traps."

Kyra had a sudden worrisome thought. "You...you weren't counting on it, were you?"

Jill looked at her for a moment, uncomprehending, and then she realized what Kyra meant. "Oh, no," she said, laughing. "No, no, no! I have no intention of getting married. Believe me, I was discouraging them with everything I could think of." She sighed, leaning back. "No, I'm a consulting geologist with an international oil company. The last thing I have in mind is being tied down to one location for any length of time. Marriage is not in the cards for me right now." She shrugged casually. "Maybe never."

"Oh, don't say that," Kyra murmured.

"Why not?" Jill smiled. "You know, I'll tell you a secret. For years after we moved to Australia, I dreamed of growing up and going back to find James, stunning him with the new beauty I was sure I would

develop someday, and marrying the poor bugger."
She threw back her head and laughed aloud. "I actually measured all my boyfriends against an ideal-
ized memory of James that I carried with me in my
heart. And, of course, they all came up wanting. I
imagine that is one reason I was driven to pursue my
career to the detriment of romance."

Kyra smiled, but with a little less enthusiasm than
before. Jill could say what she would, but she certainly had turned out beautiful. Kyra wondered what
James would think of her.

Kyra went to the kitchen and poured out glasses
of lemonade for them both, then led Jill out onto the
terrace where they sat and talked for another half
hour, until Kyra heard a key in the door and mo-
tioned for Jill to follow her back into the living room.

James came in with a frown on his face. "You
know, if they are going to change our parking area
to that side of the garage, I'm going to put the
Porsche in storage and get a tank to drive to work…"

He noticed that they had company and stopped
short, staring at Jill. His eyes widened. His mouth
opened. He tossed his keys onto the couch. "No!"
he cried, looking astonished and delighted at the
same time. "No, this can't be."

Jill stepped forward and stared at him, her eyes
dancing. "My feelings precisely," she said.

The two of them circled each other like a pair of
large cats, sizing each other up. "I can't believe it,"
they said in unison. And then they threw their arms
around each other and hugged.

Kyra watched, holding back laughter. They were
both so candidly amazed at how they'd each turned
out. They went on exclaiming over each other for

another ten minutes, and then Aunt Jo arrived and she joined in. Kyra's smile was beginning to wilt by this time. Jill was terrific. She'd liked her on sight. But she was starting to feel a little left out.

It was only natural. They hadn't seen each other for years. The best thing for her to do, she decided, was to retreat into the kitchen, leaving them to their chatter, and prepare a dinner for four. So that was what she did.

She cooked some rice, broiled a nice filet of salmon, threw together a green salad, cut up a cantaloupe, and had dinner on the table within the hour. And a darn good dinner, too, if she did say so herself. And she might as well say it, because nobody else did. They were much too busy talking and laughing and reviving old memories to notice what they were eating.

"But remember how we used to scavenge in the alleys?" Jill said, her gaze locked on James. "We were looking for bottles and cans to turn in for pennies so that we could buy Jolly Ranchers and turn our tongues green."

"I remember," James said, shaking his head at the memory and smiling. "How about that time we snuck old Mr. MacDonald's sailboat out into the bay? We got becalmed for two hours with nothing to drink and nothing to eat but a bag of potato chips. We were dying of thirst."

"Yeah," Jill responded, teasing him, "and you kept trying to recite *Rime of the Ancient Mariner* until I wanted to throw you overboard."

"Throw me overboard? I'd like to have seen you try that one."

She laughed. "Remember the time we went hiking

in the estuary and I cut my foot and you carried me all the way out?'' She smiled with obvious affection. ''You were my hero that day.''

Kyra watched all this with very mixed feelings. She knew they were old friends. She knew they should have time to go over the past without any interference from her. She knew she wasn't part of that past. When she came right down to it, she wasn't even really a part of the present—not really. But she was still getting very jealous, and she just couldn't help it. Their obvious joy in each other was beginning to hurt a little.

''So this is your nasty little freckle-faced brat, Jalopy Clark,'' she murmured to him when they were alone in the kitchen for a moment. ''With a nose like Porky Pig, if I remember correctly. I didn't recognize her from your description.''

''Hush. Don't tell her that,'' he said crossly, turning to go back out to Jill without another word.

Kyra stood where she was and fought back tears, telling herself she was being silly, but continued being silly none the less. The stupid thing was, she liked Jill. She was a wonderful woman, beautiful, accomplished, witty, and a lot of fun. If only James wouldn't look at her as though he'd just found gold.

It was late when they finally went to bed. They waited until they were sure the others were down for the night before he could slip out and go to the far bedroom, as he had been doing for the past few nights.

''She's not at all what you remember, is she?'' Kyra said to him.

He laughed softly. ''Oh, no. She's great.'' He ran a hand through his hair and smiled at her. ''Funny how I forgot all the good times and only remembered the times she drove me crazy. I'm really glad she's come. It changes everything.''

"Everything?" Kyra waited, breath held, for him to explain that terrifying statement.

But he didn't. And he didn't seem to notice that it bothered her. "I think I'll take her up to Santa Barbara tomorrow to show her Aunt Jo's house now, how it's changed. She'll get a kick out of seeing where we used to play.'' He looked at Kyra as though he'd had an afterthought. "Oh. Uh, do you want to go, too?"

She shook her head, avoiding his gaze. She didn't want him to see the hurt in her eyes. "No. No, I promised my grandmother that I'd bring her a lunch from Luigi's tomorrow. Her favorite restaurant.''

"Ah. You'd better do that, then.'' He didn't sound the least bit sorry.

"Yes," she said softly.

He listened at the door. All was quiet. Turning back to nod goodbye, he told her, "Jill is just a spectacular person, don't you think? Not what I was recalling at all.'' He shrugged and shook his head. "It is really weird to think of all that I went through...for nothing!" He gave her a "go-figure" grimace, and left the room.

And the woman he left behind stood where she was, knowing she was mortally wounded. "All that I went through...for nothing." The words echoed in her head. Tears pooled in her eyes, then splashed onto the floor. What was she going to do? What on earth could she do now?

The clock said 3 a.m. Kyra stared at it and made a decision. She hadn't slept yet and she wasn't likely to, the way her mind was racing. She'd been doing a lot of thinking, and she thought she knew what had to be done.

She'd been hired to do a job, and she'd done what had been asked of her. That job was obviously no longer necessary. It was time for her to go. James had given her a very generous advance and she'd used it to pay off most of her debts. She might have to pay him back some of that amount, but that could be worked out later. Her grandmother would have to be transferred to a cheaper facility than Avignon, but that would have been the case had she never met James Redman. There was the problem of the clothes. There were just so many outfits. Luckily, she hadn't worn most of them yet, so they could be returned. She was planning to leave with only what she'd brought with her.

But she had to stop crying first. She really shouldn't be so sad. After all, she'd had a week with James. That was more than she'd had before. A week with the man you loved wasn't much, but it had to be better than nothing at all.

Unfortunately, he wasn't made to be hers. He was made for Jill, meant for Jill from the time they were children. It had become so obvious as she'd thought about it. Jill was so right for him, and he was so happy with her. Jill was educated, sophisticated, with similar background and interests to James. And no wonder. They'd grown up together.

It was too bad, but it was reality. Her heart was broken and it hurt like hell. She had to get out of there. It was going to be awkward, but it would be pure torture to stay and watch James and Jill grow closer all the time. She wasn't brave enough to face it. Sliding out of bed, she reached for her clothes. She was going home.

James woke up and stretched and thought about Kyra. He thought about her all the time lately, about her warm brown eyes, about her honey-silk hair, about the way her breasts looked under her blue sweater, about the way she tasted.... He wanted her so badly he could hardly stand it. He writhed, tangling the covers, thinking about it. She was lying in his bed right now. What if he were to wake her up by sliding into the bed with her? It wouldn't hurt to try it.

He rolled out of bed and looked into the hallway, then made his way silently to his bedroom. He held the door so it wouldn't creak, then closed it very carefully. Finally, he turned, expecting to see Kyra's blond hair spilling out across his pillows. But what he saw was an empty bed.

His heart began to thump loudly in his chest. He went to the bathroom, but it was empty, too. The kitchen? A quick trip out into the main part of the house told him she was gone. He wasn't being careful about noise any longer. He was angry, scared and puzzled, all at the same time. After searching the last empty bedroom, he went back into his own and saw the rings on his dresser and the note beside them.

He grabbed the scrap of paper and read it quickly.

Dear James,
Now that Jill is here and has turned out so differently from what you expected, it's obvious you won't need me any longer. She's a lovely woman. I know you'll be happy together. We

can work out the financial details later. You can
send most of the clothes back. I'll pay for what
I take.

Love,

Kyra

She'd written "love" and crossed it out, then written it again. He stared down at the note, unable to
comprehend it. What the hell was she talking about?

Aunt Jo came padding into the room in her furry
slippers. He looked at her with tragic eyes, then remembered she wasn't supposed to know about
things. "I...she's gone," he said, unable to keep up
the pretense any longer. "Why would she leave like
that?"

Aunt Jo took the note from him and read it. Then
she looked piteously at her nephew. "Well, this is a
fine mess," she said. "You'd better go and get her
back."

He hesitated, avoiding her gaze. "I want to. But
it's more complicated than you know."

She threw up her hands. "James, you dunderhead!
Do you think I didn't know that you got married just
to avoid doing what I wanted you to do? All your
life you've tried to thwart me in one way or another.
You are a stubborn lad." She shook her head. "I
certainly never meant to force you to marry Jill. But
I was hoping to force you to look at your life and do
something about it."

His dark frown would have frightened a lesser
woman. "Well, I did. I got myself the perfect woman
to be my wife. But she doesn't seem to want to stay
my wife. So—"

"James Redman, are you a man or a mouse?"

He grimaced. "Good question."

"Well, you'd better answer it. How do you feel about her?"

He dug deep. It was hard to express his feelings, but he was going to try. "You know I never believed in all that love stuff. But with Kyra...you know, I really felt like I was falling in love. I didn't admit it to myself right away, but I felt it in my bones. But she kept herself so closed off to me, and I thought maybe it wasn't going to happen. Maybe she wasn't going to let it. Maybe she was going to stay so tough that I would never be able to get through to her. So I thought I'd better harden myself. And of course, that didn't work."

"Of course not. She was just protecting herself because she didn't know if she could trust you yet."

"You really think that was it?"

"Of course. It's all so simple."

"To an onlooker, maybe."

"Go after her right now, you fool," Aunt Jo lectured sternly. "She's a peach and a keeper and she's obviously in love with you."

Surprise tilted his eyebrows. "What makes you say that?"

"I've got eyes, haven't I? When I'm with her alone, she's a perfectly normal young woman. Brighter than most. But when you're around, she turns into a mass of quivering longing. She can't keep her eyes off you." She chuckled. "But that can't last forever if you abuse it. You're going to lose her if you aren't careful."

His dark frown was back. "Aunt Jo, what are you saying?"

"And here I thought you were a smart one. You love her, don't you?"

He shook his head, searching for words. "If you mean—"

"All I mean is love! Think about it. Can you stand the thought of living without her?"

He thought for only a second or two before he slowly shook his head. "No. No, I can't."

"Then you're probably in love." She patted his shoulder. "I'd go get her if I were you."

James looked at her, a smile beginning to crinkle around his eyes. "Aunt Jo. What would I do without you?"

"Forget how to feed yourself, no doubt," she muttered, shuffling back toward her room. "I'm going back to bed. I hope you have her back here by the time that I wake up." She yawned. "She makes a darn good omelet," she murmured as she disappeared into her room.

Kyra was walking sadly through the rooms of her grandmother's modest house. It seemed a somber and lonely place without her grandmother in the back bedroom. She'd only been gone herself from this place where she'd lived for so many years a little over a week, and already it didn't seem like home there any longer.

"That's because James isn't here," she sighed to herself.

Not that he'd been in this little house more than twice in his life. But she had to admit to herself, her home was now with him, wherever he was. Without him, she was always going to feel as though she didn't really belong.

What exactly was she going to do now? Go back to work, she supposed. That thought made her want to weep. How could she face everyone? How could she stand seeing James in the halls? Maybe she would have to start looking for another job.

The sound of a car in her driveway spun her around, and when she went to the front of the house to see who it was, she found James bounding up her steps.

She gasped and drew back from the window. She hadn't expected him to come after her this quickly. She wasn't ready. She didn't know what she wanted to say.

He rang the doorbell. She bit her lip, then gave up. She couldn't hide in there. But she had to make it very clear that she was being realistic. She knew the score. And she wasn't about to try to hang on to a man who didn't really want her.

Throwing open the door, she glared at him, hoping he wouldn't notice her tear-swollen eyes. "What can I do for you?" she said coolly, her hands on her hips.

He gave her that absolutely irresistible smile she loved so much. Dropping to one knee right there on her porch, he held out the diamond ring she'd left behind. "Kyra Symington, will you marry me?" he said loud and clear, in front of anyone in the neighborhood who might be looking.

She stared at him, confused. She'd expected politeness, sorrow, regret. But she'd also expected him to appreciate that she was being adult about all this, and to suggest that they get their relationship legally dissolved. Why would he confuse the issue with this phony display of...whatever this was?

"What are you talking about?" she said, shaking

her head so that her hair swirled around her face. "We're already married."

He nodded, rising from his knee a bit awkwardly, but leaning toward her without any lessening of ardor. "But as you pointed out on more than one occasion, that wedding was on paper." He grabbed her by the shoulders, looking down into her face with an intensity she recognized and loved. "What I want with you, Kyra, is a marriage of the heart."

She stared at him, afraid to hope. "Why?" she whispered.

He held her gaze with his own. "Because I love you," he said. "And I want to be with you forever."

Her knees were buckling, but that was okay, because he had her in his arms. "But, Jill—"

"I adore Jill. She's like a sister to me." He dropped a kiss on her nose. "But you are like a wife. And a good wife is hard to find."

She shook her head, not convinced. "James, wait. This is all so muddled. I'm not a real wife, I'm an employee. You pay me to…"

His gaze darkened. "Now, I'm sorry Kyra, but that is no longer in force. Here…" He pulled the contract out of his back pocket and shook it at her. "Look at this," he said, releasing her so that he could rip the contract into little pieces that floated in the air. "That is over. Gone. I refuse to pay you a penny on that contract."

She stared at him, completely at sea. "But…"

He pulled her to him again, then looked out at the street. A small knot of neighbors had gathered, whispering and nudging one another. They seemed to think this was a show put on for their benefit.

One of them even had doubts about what might be going on.

"Are you alright, Kyra?" called Harriet Klein, who lived next door. "If you want me to call the police, I'll do it right away."

"Oh." Kyra pushed out of James's embrace and went to the edge of the porch, pushing back her disheveled hair. "No, no. I'm fine, Mrs. Klein. This is—" she turned and gestured toward James "—this is my husband, everybody. We just...had a little argument." She waved at them. "Everything is fine. Nice to see you all," she called as they reluctantly began to turn away.

Grabbing James's hand, she pulled him inside and shut the door. "Now see what happened? You made a scene." She looked at his handsome face and realized she was tingling, just from being near him. "We'll be the talk of the neighborhood for weeks."

"Never mind." He pulled her to him again and kissed her firmly on the mouth. "Let them talk. We've got other things to do." He glanced around the area. "Where's your old bedroom?"

"Down the hall. Why?"

"We need to use it," he said, looking deep into her eyes. "We're going to make love." He reached down and put his arm behind her knees, lifting her effortlessly into his arms and starting down the hall.

She flung her arms around his neck to keep from flopping. "But we're not even...you tore up the contract."

"That's right," he said, kicking open the door. "We don't need it anymore."

"We don't?"

"No."

He placed her on her bed, her hair fanning out around her head, and he reached for the buttons on her blouse.

"James," she murmured, "I don't know…"

"But I do," he said, kissing her lips. "I know exactly what I'm doing." He slid his hand under her lacy bra and released it, displaying her creamy breasts in the morning light. Her rosy pink nipples contracted as he watched, making him groan with the sensation of building desire. "I'm going to make love to you until you're convinced."

"Convinced?" she said breathlessly, amazed at the way her body was responding. "Convinced of what?"

"That I love you."

"But wait…"

"What?"

She smiled up at him, tears in her eyes. But this time, they were tears of happiness. "I love you, too," she said, her voice trembling with emotion.

"Then it's official," he said, touching her lips with his finger, his heart so full of joy, he was afraid it might explode. "Goodbye, marriage on paper. Hello, marriage of the heart."

* * * * *

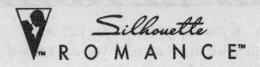

COMING NEXT MONTH

#1456 FALLING FOR GRACE—Stella Bagwell
An Older Man

The moment Jack Barrett saw his neighbor, he wanted to know everything about her. Soon he learned beautiful Grace Holliday was pregnant and alone…and too young for him. He also found out she needed protection—from *his* jaded heart....

#1457 THE BORROWED GROOM—Judy Christenberry
The Circle K Sisters

One thing held Melissa Kennedy from her dream of running a foster home—she was single. Luckily, her sexy ranch foreman, Rob Hanson, was willing to be her counterfeit fiancé, but could Melissa keep her borrowed groom…forever?

#1458 DENIM & DIAMOND—Moyra Tarling

Kyle Masters was shocked when old friend Piper Diamond asked him to marry her. He wasn't looking for a wife, yet how could he refuse when without him, she could lose custody of her unborn child? It also didn't hurt that she was a stunning beauty....

#1459 THE MONARCH'S SON—Valerie Parv
The Carramer Crown

One minute she'd washed ashore at the feet of a prince, the next, commoner Allie Carter found herself "companion" to Lorne de Marigny's son…and falling for the brooding monarch. He claimed his heart was off-limits, yet his kisses suggested something else!

#1460 JODIE'S MAIL-ORDER MAN—Julianna Morris
Bridal Fever!

Jodie Richards was sick of seeking Mr. Right, so she decided to marry her trustworthy pen pal. But when she went to meet him, she found his brother, Donovan Masters, in his place. And with one kiss, her plan for a passionless union was in danger....

#1461 LASSOED!—Martha Shields

Pose as a model for a cologne ad? That was the *last* job champion bull-rider Tucker Reeves wanted. That is, until a bull knocked him out…and Tucker woke up to lovely photographer Cassie Burch. Could she lasso this cowboy's hardened heart for good?

CMN0600

Look Who's Celebrating Our 20ᵗʰ Anniversary:

Celebrate 20 YEARS

"Happy 20ᵗʰ birthday, Silhouette. You made the writing dream of hundreds of women a reality. You enabled us to give [women] the stories [they] wanted to read and helped us teach [them] about the power of love."

—*New York Times* bestselling author
Debbie Macomber

"I wish you continued success, Silhouette Books.... Thank you for giving me a chance to do what I love best in all the world."

—International bestselling author
Diana Palmer

"A visit to Silhouette is a guaranteed happy ending, a chance to touch magic for a little while.... It refreshes and revitalizes and makes us feel better.... I hope Silhouette goes on forever."

—Award-winning bestselling author
Marie Ferrarella

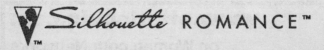

Silhouette ROMANCE™

SILHOUETTE'S 20TH ANNIVERSARY CONTEST
OFFICIAL RULES
NO PURCHASE NECESSARY TO ENTER

1. To enter, follow directions published in the offer to which you are responding. Contest begins 1/1/00 and ends on 8/24/00 (the "Promotion Period"). Method of entry may vary. Mailed entries must be postmarked by 8/24/00, and received by 8/31/00.

2. During the Promotion Period, the Contest may be presented via the Internet. Entry via the Internet may be restricted to residents of certain geographic areas that are disclosed on the Web site. To enter via the Internet, if you are a resident of a geographic area in which Internet entry is permissible, follow the directions displayed on-line, including typing your essay of 100 words or fewer telling us "Where In The World Your Love Will Come Alive." On-line entries must be received by 11:59 p.m. Eastern Standard time on 8/24/00. Limit one e-mail entry per person, household and e-mail address per day, per presentation. If you are a resident of a geographic area in which entry via the Internet is permissible, you may, in lieu of submitting an entry on-line, enter by mail, by hand-printing your name, address, telephone number and contest number/name on an 8"x 11" plain piece of paper and telling us in 100 words or fewer "Where In The World Your Love Will Come Alive," and mailing via first-class mail to: Silhouette 20th Anniversary Contest, (in the U.S.) P.O. Box 9069, Buffalo, NY 14269-9069; (In Canada) P.O. Box 637, Fort Erie, Ontario, Canada L2A 5X3. Limit one 8"x 11" mailed entry per person, household and e-mail address per day. On-line and/or 8"x 11" mailed entries received from persons residing in geographic areas in which Internet entry is not permissible will be disqualified. No liability is assumed for lost, late, incomplete, inaccurate, nondelivered or misdirected mail, or misdirected e-mail, for technical, hardware or software failures of any kind, lost or unavailable network connection, or failed, incomplete, garbled or delayed computer transmission or any human error which may occur in the receipt or processing of the entries in the contest.

3. Essays will be judged by a panel of members of the Silhouette editorial and marketing staff based on the following criteria:

   Sincerity (believability, credibility)—50%

   Originality (freshness, creativity)—30%

   Aptness (appropriateness to contest ideas)—20%

   Purchase or acceptance of a product offer does not improve your chances of winning. In the event of a tie, duplicate prizes will be awarded.

4. All entries become the property of Harlequin Enterprises Ltd., and will not be returned. Winner will be determined no later than 10/31/00 and will be notified by mail. Grand Prize winner will be required to sign and return Affidavit of Eligibility within 15 days of receipt of notification. Noncompliance within the time period may result in disqualification and an alternative winner may be selected. All municipal, provincial, federal, state and local laws and regulations apply. Contest open only to residents of the U.S. and Canada who are 18 years of age or older, and is void wherever prohibited by law. Internet entry is restricted solely to residents of those geographical areas in which Internet entry is permissible. Employees of Torstar Corp., their affiliates, agents and members of their immediate families are not eligible. Taxes on the prizes are the sole responsibility of winners. Entry and acceptance of any prize offered constitutes permission to use winner's name, photograph or other likeness for the purposes of advertising, trade and promotion on behalf of Torstar Corp. without further compensation to the winner, unless prohibited by law. Torstar Corp and D.L. Blair, Inc., their parents, affiliates and subsidiaries, are not responsible for errors in printing or electronic presentation of contest or entries. In the event of printing or other errors which may result in unintended prize values or duplication of prizes, all affected contest materials or entries shall be null and void. If for any reason the Internet portion of the contest is not capable of running as planned, including infection by computer virus, bugs, tampering, unauthorized intervention, fraud, technical failures, or any other causes beyond the control of Torstar Corp. which corrupt or affect the administration, secrecy, fairness, integrity or proper conduct of the contest, Torstar Corp. reserves the right, at its sole discretion, to disqualify any individual who tampers with the entry process and to cancel, terminate, modify or suspend the contest or the Internet portion thereof. In the event of a dispute regarding an on-line entry, the entry will be deemed submitted by the authorized holder of the e-mail account submitted at the time of entry. Authorized account holder is defined as the natural person who is assigned to an e-mail address by an Internet access provider, on-line service provider or other organization that is responsible for arranging e-mail address for the domain associated with the submitted e-mail address.

5. Prizes: Grand Prize—a $10,000 vacation to anywhere in the world. Travelers (at least one must be 18 years of age or older) or parent or guardian if one traveler is a minor, must sign and return a Release of Liability prior to departure. Travel must be completed by December 31, 2001, and is subject to space and accommodations availability. Two hundred (200) Second Prizes—a two-book limited edition autographed collector set from one of the Silhouette Anniversary authors: Nora Roberts, Diana Palmer, Linda Howard or Annette Broadrick (value $10.00 each set). All prizes are valued in U.S. dollars.

6. For a list of winners (available after 10/31/00), send a self-addressed, stamped envelope to: Harlequin Silhouette 20th Anniversary Winners, P.O. Box 4200, Blair, NE 68009-4200.

Contest sponsored by Torstar Corp., P.O. Box 9042, Buffalo, NY 14269-9042.

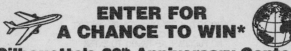

ENTER FOR A CHANCE TO WIN*

Silhouette's 20th Anniversary Contest

Tell Us Where in the World You Would Like *Your* Love To Come Alive... And We'll Send the Lucky Winner There!

Silhouette wants to take you wherever your happy ending can come true.

Here's how to enter: Tell us, in 100 words or less, where you want to go to make your love come alive!

In addition to the grand prize, there will be 200 runner-up prizes, collector's-edition book sets autographed by one of the Silhouette anniversary authors: **Nora Roberts, Diana Palmer, Linda Howard** or **Annette Broadrick.**

DON'T MISS YOUR CHANCE TO WIN! ENTER NOW! No Purchase Necessary

Where love comes alive™

Visit Silhouette at www.eHarlequin.com to enter, starting this summer.

Name: _____

Address: _____

City: _____ State/Province: _____

Zip/Postal Code: _____

Mail to Harlequin Books: **In the U.S.:** P.O. Box 9069, Buffalo, NY 14269-9069; **In Canada:** P.O. Box 637, Fort Erie, Ontario, L4A 5X3

*No purchase necessary—for contest details send a self-addressed stamped envelope to: Silhouette's 20th Anniversary Contest, P.O. Box 9069, Buffalo, NY, 14269-9069 (include contest name on self-addressed envelope). Residents of Washington and Vermont may omit postage. Open to Cdn. (excluding Quebec) and U.S. residents who are 18 or over. Void where prohibited. Contest ends August 31, 2000.   PS20CON_R2